THE KILLER IN THE CHOIR

A Selection of Recent Titles by Simon Brett

The Fethering Mysteries

BONES UNDER THE BEACH HUT
GUNS IN THE GALLERY *
THE CORPSE ON THE COURT *
THE STRANGLING ON THE STAGE *
THE TOMB IN TURKEY *
THE KILLING IN THE CAFÉ *
THE LIAR IN THE LIBRARY *
THE KILLER IN THE CHOIR *

The Charles Paris Theatrical Series

A RECONSTRUCTED CORPSE
SICKEN AND SO DIE
DEAD ROOM FARCE
A DECENT INTERVAL *
THE CINDERELLA KILLER *
A DEADLY HABIT *

The Mrs Pargeter Mysteries

MRS PARGETER'S PACKAGE
MRS PARGETER'S POUND OF FLESH
MRS PARGETER'S PLOT
MRS PARGETER'S POINT OF HONOUR
MRS PARGETER'S PRINCIPLE *
MRS PARGETER'S PUBLIC RELATIONS *

* *available from Severn House*

THE KILLER IN THE CHOIR

Simon Brett

Severn House Large Print
London & New York

This first large print edition published 2020
in Great Britain and the USA by
SEVERN HOUSE PUBLISHERS LTD of
Eardley House, 4 Uxbridge Street, London W8 7SY.
First world regular print edition published 2019 by
Severn House Publishers Ltd.

British Library Cataloguing in Publication Data
A CIP catalogue record for this title is available from the British Library.

ISBN-13: 9780727892393

Typeset by Palimpsest Book Production Ltd.,
Falkirk, Stirlingshire, Scotland.
Printed and bound in Great Britain by
T J International, Padstow, Cornwall.

To the hope that,
in my next incarnation,
I'll be able to sing

EPITAPH ON AN AMATEUR SOPRANO

Her final note has now been sent,
Her final chord's undone.
After life's gloom, death should present
Her moment in the sun.
Alas, she has the worst of fates –
She must in Limbo stay
And wait outside the Pearly Gates
For ever and a day.
She's not shut out because of sin.
Her virtue's plain to see.
It's just . . . she never knew when to come in,
And could never find the key.

One

The trouble is, thought Carole Seddon peevishly, that no one knows any of the old hymns any more. Though devoutly anti-religious, she did have standards when it came to certain matters of British tradition. And she was strongly of the view that children should be brought up to know the basic repertory of hymn tunes that she'd had to learn at their age.

Carole was not a frequent visitor to All Saints Church in the village of Fethering. Lack of faith precluded regular Sunday attendance and, as a divorced woman in her fifties, she was not invited to many weddings or christenings. So, it was just funerals, really. And it was a funeral that had brought her to All Saints that Thursday morning in late February.

She had not known the deceased, Leonard Mallett, well, nor liked him very much. Of his professional career, in the world of insurance, she knew nothing. But they had both been on the same committee, which he had chaired, for the Preservation of Fethering's Seafront. Though the group only met a couple of times a year, Carole had found out through the local grapevine that most of the other members would be attending the funeral. So, after the disproportionate amount of soul-searching that she brought to every social situation, she'd decided she ought to join them. Though Leonard himself was obviously beyond being offended, and Carole hardly knew his wife Heather, she still felt the danger that her absence might be interpreted as some kind of snub (unaware of the more likely truth that it simply wouldn't be noticed).

So, she was there in the church. Though there are many beautiful old churches in West Sussex, some dating back to Saxon times, All Saints Fethering was not one of them. It had been built by the Victorians in dour dark red brick and seemed somehow too high and cavernous ever to feel welcoming. As with every such institution in the country, the age of its dwindling congregation mounted with each passing year, and there didn't seem to be many young people leaping in to replace those called to a Higher Place.

Leonard Mallett's funeral, however, had very nearly filled the church. Despite arriving characteristically early, Carole had been ushered into one of the side pews. This vantage point, though not in the favoured central block, gave her a good view of the altar and choir stalls, and of the trestles on which the deceased's coffin would shortly rest.

At the door, she had been handed an order of service. A quick glance through its contents revealed no surprises. The hymns were totally predictable. As were the readings, even down to the inevitability of Joyce Grenfell's 'If I should die before the rest of you' and Henry Scott Holland's one about having 'slipped away to the next room'. (Carole had nothing against either of them as poems; she just wished people might occasionally choose something else. But funerals were rare and stressful events for most people, so perhaps it was too much to hope for originality.)

On the order of service's cover there was a colour photograph of Leonard Mallett. Characteristically unsmiling, he wore the frustrated expression of a man who wasn't at that moment getting his own way. It was not a face that inspired affection.

But something about the man had inspired the healthy turnout for his funeral. There were a few Fethering regulars, some members of the Seafront committee, to whom Carole gave minimal nodding acknowledgement, but most of the congregation were unfamiliar to her. Presumably people from Leonard's former London life, senior managers from the world of insurance, who had ventured down to the South Coast to pay their dutiful respects in the forbidding draughtiness of All Saints Fethering.

Somehow, to Carole, the church's bleak austerity felt appropriate for the funeral of someone she had hardly known.

In Fethering, of course, the fact that you hardly knew someone didn't mean that you were totally ignorant of their circumstances. Gossip could be relied on to generate an extensive dossier, based on some fact and much conjecture, about every resident of that South Coast village. And, although Carole had received none of the information from the man himself, she knew that Heather was Leonard Mallett's second wife, though it was a first marriage for her. They'd had no children together, but he had a daughter with his first wife, who had subsequently died (though nobody knew exactly when). The girl was called Alice. She was rumoured to be an actress who didn't get much work, but who lived quite comfortably in London on an allowance from her father.

Fethering gossip had it that Alice was engaged to be married. It also said that she didn't get on with her stepmother. Though there was evidence about the forthcoming wedding, because it was due to take place at All Saints, the bit about tensions between the two women was pure speculation. But then Fethering gossip always tended to go for the rather simplistic fairy-tale interpretation of family relationships. It wouldn't entertain the idea of a stepmother and stepdaughter who got on well together.

Leonard Mallett was said to have been some fifteen years older than his second wife. He had moved to the village, into a large house called Sorrento on the exclusive Shorelands Estate, towards the end of a long and lucrative career bossing people about in insurance. After a few years of daily commuting to London, he had devoted his retirement to bossing people about in Fethering. It was on his initiative that the Preservation of Fethering's Seafront committee had been set up, and the fact that he had persuaded Carole Seddon, not by nature a joiner of anything, to become a member, was a measure of his bossing skills.

She had not enjoyed his hectoring manner at meetings, but could not fault the fact that he had set up the committee. On her morning walks with her Labrador, Gulliver, she had become increasingly aware of the pollution affecting Fethering

Beach. Every day's tides deposited more tar-soiled plastic items on the shoreline. And tourists seemed deliberately to avoid the litter bins on the prom, preferring to scatter their burger boxes, polystyrene chip trays and ice-cream wrappers directly on to the ground. As she grew older, and perhaps since she had been blessed with two granddaughters, Carole had become increasingly worried about the legacy of pollution being bequeathed to future generations.

Fethering gossip's dossier on Heather Mallett was less detailed than the one it had compiled on her husband. This was in part because she was rarely seen around the village. Though Leonard was a constant and loud presence at all Fethering events, and particularly in its only pub, the Crown & Anchor, his wife kept herself to herself. She was rarely to be seen shopping on the Parade. Presumably, she favoured the large anonymous supermarkets, like Sainsbury's in Rustington, over the local outlets. The only guaranteed sightings of her in the village were at church on Sundays, and at Friday rehearsals for the All Saints choir, of which she was a diligent member.

Heather Mallett was a pallid creature, who favoured anonymous colours: beige, light pinks and taupe. Though probably about the same age as Carole, she had the resigned air of a woman who did not expect post-menopausal life to yield any excitements. Unlike Carole, whose hair had been cut in the same helmet shape since schooldays when it was dark brown until now when it was grey, Heather's hair, that pale blonde which edges almost imperceptibly into white, was cut very short. Like Carole, she usually wore undistinguished rimless glasses.

That was the first thing about her at the funeral that looked odd. In place of the familiar, almost transparent pair, Heather Mallett was wearing glasses with thick, oxblood-coloured frames. They looked almost fashionable, and certainly emphasized the rather fine brown eyes which nobody had ever noticed before. She had let her hair grow longer too. And the black trouser suit she wore was almost 'sharp', making a definite change from her normal dowdy appearance.

The other odd thing that morning in All Saints was that Heather Mallett did not follow the coffin into the church, in the customary manner of a newly bereaved widow. Nor did she subsequently take her place in the front pew, attended by sympathetic family members. Instead, she had entered earlier, with the rest of the choir, all of whom wore their usual clothes rather than cassocks. Following someone's directive – possibly the widow's – they had not 'robed' for the occasion.

The line-up of the choir was predictable. Obviously – and inevitably – more women than men, and women whose average age was pushing seventy. The youngest female members were an acne-plagued teenage girl and a thin, tough-looking woman in her forties. The girl Carole recognized from behind the till at Allinstore, Fethering's uniquely inefficient supermarket. The woman she did not know, which, given the way the village worked, probably meant she came from elsewhere or was a recent arrival.

The male components comprised two. There was a bustling, bearded man in his early seventies, whom Carole did actually know. He was a retired schoolteacher called Ruskin Dewitt, who had also been a member of Leonard Mallett's Preservation of Fethering's Seafront committee. The other male was a boy enduring the aching awkwardness of early adolescence, whose main aim in life seemed to be not to catch the eye of the Allinstore checkout girl. So deficient was the choir in male voices that the church organist, whose name Carole happened to know was Jonny Virgo, joined lustily in all the singing.

As did Heather Mallett. Which still seemed odd to Carole. She supposed that, for someone to whom singing the praises of God was important, to do so might feel like the best tribute one could bring to the celebration of a husband's life. But it still didn't feel quite right. Carole disliked witnessing any divergence from the conventions and rituals that she didn't believe in.

Nor was she the only person registering disapproval. In the front pew, next to the aisle, in the seat which might have been considered the rightful place of the widow, sat the deceased's daughter, Alice Mallett. Though Fethering gossip placed her in her early thirties, she had the look of a recalcitrant schoolgirl. The loose black dress she wore failed to disguise her dumpiness, and the black straw Zorro-style sombrero had not been a good fashion choice.

Beside her sat a tall man of matching dumpiness, dressed in conventional pin-striped suit and black tie. His attentiveness to his companion suggested that he might be the fiancé Fethering gossip had announced Alice Mallett was about to marry. Regrettably, the full resources of the Fethering grapevine had not been able to come up with a name for him.

The All Saints choir was in place by the time the coffin entered, accompanied by Jonny Virgo the organist's expert playing of Bach's 'Cantata No. 208 Sheep May Safely Graze'. The chief undertaker, in his tall black hat at the front of the procession, appeared to be enjoying his master-of-ceremonies role, and the pall-bearers looked more as if they were his employees than dignitaries of the insurance world.

As they lowered the coffin on to its waiting trestles, the vicar moved into position in front of the altar and requested that the congregation remain standing for the first hymn, predictably enough, 'The Day Thou Gavest, Lord, is Ended'.

'. . . and the fact that we are all gathered here to see Leonard off on his final journey shows how much he meant to every one of us.'

Carole found the vicar's words arguable. She certainly wasn't in All Saints because the deceased had meant much to her. And looking round at the other attendees, she didn't reckon he had figured a great deal in their affections either. It was just social convention, not any genuine emotion, that had brought them all out for the funeral. (Very occasionally, Carole Seddon worried that her cynicism about the motivation of her fellow human beings was increasing, but she could quickly reassure herself by observation of their behaviour, which showed no signs of improving.)

'Leonard,' the vicar went on, 'was very successful in his professional career, in the world of insurance, and I am delighted to welcome many of his former colleagues to All Saints today for this . . . celebration of his life. When he moved down here to Fethering, he did not just put his feet up, as many retired people seem to do. He entered thoroughly into the affairs of our community, bringing those organizational skills which had served him so well in his business life, into "doing his bit" for our village. It was Leonard who set up a committee for the Preservation of Fethering's Seafront, and he did sterling work in . . .'

It was clear to Carole that, as was so often the case with contemporary funerals, the celebrant knew nothing about the person whose departure his church was hosting. Maybe the two had met through Heather's connection with the choir, but Leonard Mallett had resolutely not been a church-goer. Clearly, the two men had spent very little time together.

Apart from anything else, the vicar was relatively new to the Parish of All Saints. Of course, the dearth of church-goers in Fethering did not mean that his arrival had passed unnoticed by the wider village community. He had already been much discussed and commented on, before and after he took up the post. Lack of interest in religion in no way precluded interest in a new vicar, which in a small village reached almost Jane Austen proportions.

Carole reviewed the dossier which Fethering

gossip had already compiled on him. The Reverend Bob Hinkley had not spent his entire career in the church. He had worked 'in industry' and 'apparently been quite high up', though nobody could specify what industry he had been in, or how high up he had been in it. But he was said to have had a 'Damascene conversion' in his early fifties and decided then to train for holy orders. The career change had caused him, everyone agreed, 'a serious loss of income'.

To the acquisitive minds of Fethering, this was definitely a bad thing. But perhaps not such a bad thing for Bob Hinkley as it might have been for most people. Because Bob Hinkley was rumoured to have 'a rich wife'. It was here that the contents of the Fethering gossip dossier became rather sketchy. Because nobody had actually met his rich wife.

Since this largely invented person was not sharing the vicarage with her husband, the locals, once again going for the obvious explanation, deduced that there was 'something wrong with the marriage'. The sages of the Crown & Anchor even speculated further that his wife wanted a divorce, but Bob wouldn't entertain the idea because it didn't fit his image as a man of the cloth, particularly one recently arrived in a new parish. Speculation in Fethering, as ever, had only a nodding acquaintance with the truth. When the village residents got better acquainted with the new vicar, no doubt his dossier would grow bigger and, hopefully, more accurate. They would even find out that he didn't have a wife, rich or otherwise.

'So,' the droning encomium continued, 'as our brother Leonard moves on from this world to a better one, it is with the comforting knowledge that he lived a fulfilling and useful life . . .'

Carole's cynicism struck again. How could Bob Hinkley possibly know that? How could anyone ever be sure what actually went on in another person's life? From what she'd seen of Leonard Mallett, he gave the impression of being a complete bastard.

She knew the All Saints church hall quite well. There were few rentable public spaces in Fethering, so it was impossible to live in the village for long without having to attend some function at the venue. And though it was regularly maintained by the local council, the space never felt welcoming. Each repainting of the interior favoured the same cream and pale green paint and, even when bunting was hung out for wedding receptions, or lametta for Christmas parties, the hall remained resolutely institutional. Appropriate, perhaps, for the wake after a funeral of someone you hadn't known well, or particularly liked.

It was not natural sociability that prompted Carole to go to the church hall. Her instinct would have been to head straight from All Saints back to her house, High Tor, but her curiosity proved stronger. There was something about the Mallett family set-up that intrigued her. Maybe it was just Heather's glasses and longer hair, a suggestion that the invisible woman of Fethering was about to become more conspicuous.

If that was happening, the process was clearly

continuing at her husband's wake. By the time Carole arrived in the hall, Heather was already quaffing champagne and laughing extravagantly in the centre of a group of her church choir cronies. Perhaps it was sheer relief at the end of the ceremony, or a complex reaction to the grief of bereavement, but Heather Mallett seemed to have slipped very easily into Merry Widow mode.

One of the group Carole recognized was the church organist, who had so vigorously played and sung throughout the ceremony. On the authority of Fethering gossip, Jonny Virgo had relatively recently retired as Head of Music at some local school, where he had, as throughout his own education and subsequent career, suffered many jokes at the expense of his surname. He lived with his mother, now well into her nineties, in one of the old fishermen's cottages down near Fethering Yacht Club. Whenever this fact was mentioned by Fethering gossips, it was done with a raised eyebrow, an implicit comment on his likely sexuality. But Jonny Virgo was believed never to have had a partner, of any gender. Nor had any scandal ever attached to his name.

Carole noticed that he stood rather awkwardly, as though he were in pain, on the fringe of Heather Mallett's entourage. He wore a dull brown suit, and at the neck of his white shirt a cravat of a maroon paisley design, a slightly dated gesture to leisurewear. But the choirmaster seemed very much part of the communal jollity. Carole felt the instinctive recoil she did from any kind of hearty group dynamic. She never felt relaxed in the company of more than one person – and very rarely even then.

There hadn't been anyone with filled glasses on trays to greet the guests arriving from the church, and Carole didn't yet want to join the throng at the drinks table over by the serving hatch to the kitchen. She really felt like a glass of wine, but knew she'd probably end up with a cup of coffee. It wasn't even twelve o'clock yet. She didn't want to get a reputation. And reputations were easily acquired in Fethering.

Carole checked out the crowd for other familiar faces. It was a local routine that she knew well. All that was needed at an occasion like this was one person with whom you had previously exchanged dialogue. Although everyone in the village knew to the last detail exactly who everyone else in the village was, to introduce yourself directly was not considered good form. The correct procedure was to start talking to someone you'd talked to before, in the hope that they would then introduce you to people you hadn't talked to before. And then, at the next awkward village event, you would have a wider acquaintance with whom you could initiate conversation. And so, in theory, your social circle expanded.

Carole looked round desperately for any fellow members of the Preservation of Fethering's Seafront committee, apart from Ruskin Dewitt, who had looked straight through her, as if they'd never met before. She couldn't see any others. Maybe they all felt that they'd done their bit by turning up at the church, and that attending the wake too was beyond the call of duty.

Rather than standing there, exposed as someone who didn't know anybody, Carole was about to slip away back to High Tor when she was greeted by a bonhomous cry of, 'Hello. Bloody good service, wasn't it?'

The voice came from the tall young man, dressed in a pin-striped suit and wearing an appropriate black tie, who had accompanied Alice Mallett in the church. He had the red face of someone who spent a lot of time outdoors, and the figure of a fit young man who was just starting to go to fat.

Carole was faced by another social dilemma. She was sure she knew who the speaker was, but she hadn't been properly introduced and only had Fethering gossip as her guide. 'Yes, very good service,' she said clumsily. 'I'm sorry? Do we know each other?'

'No, but since I know hardly anyone here, I thought I should jolly well take the initiative.'

'Very good idea.' There was a silence. 'I'm sorry. I still don't know who you are.'

'Ah. Right. Roddy Skelton.'

'Oh.' But still Fethering etiquette did not allow her to say, 'You're Alice Mallett's fiancé.'

Fortunately, he supplied the deficiency by saying, 'I'm Alice Mallett's fiancé. Had her old man waited a bit longer before he kicked the bucket, I'd be able to say I was his son-in-law.'

'Ah yes. Well, nice to meet you. I'm Carole Seddon.'

'Old friend of the family?'

'Hardly. That is to say, I met your father-in

– your prospective father-in-law – through a committee he set up.'

'Ah.' After the initial burst, the conversation seemed to have become becalmed.

'About the Preservation of Fethering's Seafront,' Carole volunteered.

'Oh yes, good stuff. All have a responsibility for the countryside, don't we?'

'Certainly.'

'Mustn't forget it.' Then he said randomly, as people always did in this kind of conversation, 'Global warming, eh?'

'So . . .' Carole picked up after a long pause, 'when are you and Alice actually getting married?'

'Seventeenth of May.'

'Ah. Here?'

'Yes. Traditional stuff. We're both locals, well, we were. Alice, of course, hoped her old man would be able to walk her up the aisle, but . . . well, there you go . . .'

'Mm.'

The next silence that threatened was interrupted by the approach of Roddy's fiancée. Alice Mallett was holding a flute into which she was pouring from a bottle of champagne. 'Hello,' she said in a voice that suggested she'd downed an unfeasible number of drinks since the wake started or, more likely, had got some in before the ceremony.

'Steady on, old thing,' said Roddy, indicating the glass. 'You're meant to be one of the hostesses here, you know. Pouring drinks and things.'

'I am pouring drinks.'

'Yes, but you're meant to be pouring drinks

for other people, not just yourself.' He guffawed, somewhat unnaturally, trying to sound as if he was making a joke. But the look he gave his fiancée suggested genuine concern.

Alice Mallett stared at their empty hands. 'You haven't got glasses. I can't pour for you if you haven't got glasses.'

'But maybe you could—'

'Shut up, Roddy! I'm being more of a bloody hostess than *she* is.' She jutted a contemptuous shoulder towards her stepmother.

'Now come on, sweetie,' said Roddy in a conciliatory tone which Carole felt might get used a lot in the course of his upcoming marriage, 'today's about your old man, not about Heather.'

'Is it?' demanded his fiancée combatively. She turned suddenly to Carole. 'Do you like her?'

'Sorry? Who?' She knew the answer, was merely playing for time.

'Her. Heather. My stepmother.'

'I've never really met her properly.'

'Very sensible. Keep it that way, if you've got any sense.'

'Oh?' Carole was bemused by this sudden aggression.

'Well, I've met her properly,' Alice continued. 'I've spent much longer with her than I would ever wish to have done. And I don't like her.'

'No, I rather got that impression,' said Carole.

'As a general rule,' came the acid response, 'people don't tend to like the woman who's killed their father.'

Two

Carole left the wake without having a drink, either coffee or champagne. After making her astonishing statement, the bereaved – and very drunk – stepdaughter had moved away, with her fiancé fussing at her side, trying to get her to behave more appropriately. Carole had another quick look around to see if there was anyone she wanted to talk to, and finding with no great surprise that there wasn't, slipped unobtrusively out of the hall and returned to High Tor.

As she entered the kitchen, her Labrador Gulliver looked up from his station in front of the Aga. His expression was, as ever, hopeful, though he knew he had already had his morning outing on Fethering Beach, and no other walks would be on offer until early evening.

Carole was in a dilemma. She desperately wanted to share what Alice Mallett had said with her neighbour, Jude, but she never went the easy way around any social interaction. Had she lived in the North of England – or indeed had she been a less uptight Southerner – she would have gone straight next door to Woodside Cottage to see if her friend was in. But Carole, being Carole, phoned instead.

Jude was in. 'How did the funeral go?' she asked.

'Very interesting.'

'Oh?'

'I'd love to talk to you about it.'

'Talk away. I am in listening mode.'

'Well, I wondered if we could meet . . .?'

Jude couldn't entirely keep a giggle out of her voice as she said, 'Given our proximity, I'd say that was quite possible.'

'Yes. Well . . . you wouldn't fancy joining me for lunch at the Crown & Anchor, would you?' This was unusual. It was rare for Carole to suggest a pub visit in the middle of the day.

Jude's response was unusual too. She said, 'No.'

'Oh?'

'Sorry, I've got a client booked in at two.'

'Ah.' The monosyllable managed to convey all of Carole's reservations about her neighbour's work as a healer.

'Trouble is, it seems a bit pointless going to the pub and not having a drink, but I do need my concentration to be . . .'

'Of course. Well, how about you coming round here? I could assemble a salad . . .'

'Hmm,' said Jude, when Carole had finished her report on the wake. She pushed aside her empty plate and shook her bird's nest of blonde hair. 'Emotions tend to run high at that kind of occasion.'

'Of course.'

'And if, as you say, there was already a legacy of bad blood between stepdaughter and stepmother . . .'

'So Fethering gossip has it.'

'Never underestimate Fethering gossip, Carole.

It's almost always hopelessly wrong on detail, but it often gets the main outlines right.'

'Yes.'

'The daughter . . . Alice did you say?'

'Mm.'

'She doesn't live down here?'

'No. London, I think.'

'I've never met her. Nor the mother . . . Heather . . . I don't think I'd even recognize her.'

'She's very rarely seen around the village.'

'Oh?'

'Just church on Sundays and church choir rehearsals on Fridays.'

'Ah. Where do they – well, where does she – live?'

'Shorelands Estate.'

'Say no more. That lot are always a bit up themselves, aren't they?'

It was true. Shorelands was one of those private estates, not quite gated, but with controlled access. The houses were overlarge, trumpeting their owners' wealth, and each one built in a different architectural style. The Shorelands Estate was the kind of place where there were regulations about which days you could put your washing out. And where you could walk your dogs. And when you could mow your lawns.

'Of course, "killing" . . .' Carole began.

'Hm?'

'Well, I was just going to say . . . "killing" could mean a lot of things.'

'As in Heather Mallett's having "killed" her husband?'

'Exactly. From an aggrieved – and bereaved

– stepdaughter . . . it could be kind of metaphorical.'

'"You killed my father by making his life a misery" . . . that kind of thing?'

'Yes.'

'"You killed my father by feeding him lots of fatty food" . . . or by "stopping him from going to the doctor when he felt ill" . . .?'

'Mm.'

'Infinite possibilities.'

'It could also, of course mean . . .' began Carole cautiously, 'that Alice was actually accusing Heather of murdering her stepfather . . .?'

Jude grinned wryly. 'I wondered how long it would take you to get there.'

'Well, it's possible.'

'Undoubtedly. Unlikely, but possible. And do we know how Leonard Mallett was supposed to have died?'

'No.'

'Because information about that might help us to establish the viability of the murder hypothesis.'

'Yes.' Carole looked at her neighbour suspiciously. Lacking a robust sense of humour, she was never quite sure when she was being sent up.

'Well, Carole,' said Jude with a grin, 'if you hear any more about the murder of Leonard Mallett, you will keep me up to speed about it, won't you?'

'Of course. And you'll do the same?'

'I will share every last piece of incriminating evidence with you,' promised Jude. She looked at her watch. It had a large round face and was tied to her wrist with a kind of ribbon. This idiosyncrasy always irked Carole. She thought watches ought to be discreetly small, with proper straps. 'Better be going,' said Jude. 'As I said, client coming at two.'

'Oh yes. Of course,' said Carole, her scepticism once again evident about the whole business of healing.

It was not the first time Jude had treated Jonny Virgo. She hadn't mentioned the name of her two o'clock booking to her neighbour. She had strict rules about client confidentiality.

She knew about Jonny's past career as Head of Music at a school called Ravenhall, but he'd never before mentioned that he played the organ at All Saints. As soon as he said he'd just come from post-funeral drinks, though, she made the connection.

'I went to the Seaview Café to get some lunch,' he confided. 'There were only nibbles in the church hall after the ceremony. And, you know, I have to have regular meals. Because of my blood sugar.'

Jonny Virgo's 'blood sugar' was a much-discussed topic. From an early age, his mother had made him aware of the importance of keeping up the right level of blood sugar in his body, and from this he had developed a paranoia about the dangers of missing meals. He had a good few other paranoias about his health, mostly related to digestion. The easy diagnosis of Jonny Virgo's condition would be hypochondria.

But Jude looked deeper than that. She knew,

from what he had said to her, that Jonny had tried all kinds of conventional medicines and alternative therapies for his many ailments before he had approached her. She found him a challenge, and one that she wanted to prove equal to. Yes, a lot of the symptoms he described were psychosomatic, but there was some genuine malaise at the centre of it all. Jude did not believe in separating physical and mental illness. She knew how inextricably intertwined they were, and her aim was always to heal the whole person.

The one unarguably genuine ailment that Jonny Virgo suffered from was a bad back. Her practice had taught Jude that a lot of bad backs were more in the head than in the muscles, but Jonny's was the real thing. It had been caused, he admitted, by a lifetime of piano playing, both practising by himself and teaching. All those long hours of sitting on a stool with no back support had taken their toll. Jude could tell from the tightness of his muscles, particularly in the lower back area, how much concentration he put into his work at the keyboard, channelling the works of the world's great composers. She knew that the only prospect of a cure for his pain was for him to give up playing, but she also knew that that was the one solution she could not suggest. Playing the piano was what defined Jonny Virgo to himself. It was not only the work that had always been at the centre of his life; it was also his favoured means of release. Playing piano relaxed him.

And he needed some form of relaxation. Jude had gathered, in previous sessions, that caring for his elderly mother was very stressful. Though he didn't mention the word, the old lady was clearly on the slide towards dementia. 'She can't remember what she said two minutes ago, but she still loves hearing me play the piano,' he kept saying. 'She says hearing me play makes her very peaceful. I can't stop playing because of Mother, apart from anything else. It wouldn't be fair on her.'

So, Jude recognized that she could never cure his pain, only offer him ways to manage it.

Jonny knew the routine. He took off his jacket and shoes, removed the cravat from around his neck and lay face down on the treatment bed which Jude had put up in her sitting room. On first moving into Woodside Cottage, she had contemplated having a dedicated area for her healing work, but decided – rightly, as it turned out – that her clients would be more relaxed in the charming disorder of her living space. Jude's style of décor reflected the clothes she wore. Just as a variety of floaty garments blurred the exact outline of her plumpness, so a range of rugs, throws and floppy cushions disguised the contours of her furniture. Carole had never actually vocalized her views on the organized chaos in which her neighbour lived, but Jude knew full well what she thought. She gloried in the contrast between the soft confusion of Woodside Cottage and the sharp edges of High Tor's immaculate interior.

The interest in crime-solving that she and Carole shared had occasionally presented Jude with ethical dilemmas in relation to her work. More than once it had happened that a client had been deeply involved in an investigation, either as a research source, a witness or, on occasion, a perpetrator. Jude tried not to use her confidential healer role as a means of eliciting information, but sometimes the strain told. And, after what Carole had reported from Leonard Mallett's wake, the temptation to pick Jonny Virgo's brains was strong.

She needn't have worried, though. As she moved her hands slowly up and down, a few inches above his body, focusing her concentration on its messages, with absolutely no prompting the organist went straight to the subject that interested her.

'Very strange,' he confided. 'Obviously I've done a lot of funerals in my time, and I'm not sure that they're occasions when you necessarily see the best of human behaviour, particularly after everyone's had a few drinks, but what happened today was completely unprecedented.'

'Oh?' said Jude, as if just making conversation.

'The deceased was a Fethering resident called Leonard Mallett . . . don't know if you knew him?'

'I've heard the name,' she replied with complete honesty.

'Lived in one of those big houses over on the Shorelands Estate.'

'Ah. Did you know him?'

'Not really. His wife – widow I have to say now – sings in the church choir. I'd seen him once or twice coming to pick her up, that's all. She's a soprano,' he added randomly.

'Oh.'

'And one strange thing that happened today was that, during the service, rather than sitting with the congregation, she sat in the choir stalls and sang along with the rest of them.'

'Well, I suppose that was her choice,' said Jude, wondering if there was going to come a point when Jonny added more to the narrative than she'd already heard from Carole.

'Oh yes, yes. And I was very happy about it. Quite honestly, we're so pushed for numbers in the choir that I worry about anyone's absence – even if they've got the excuse of it being their husband's funeral. Some of the more traditional members of the All Saints congregation might have seen it as a little lacking in respect, but as you say, it was her choice. And she's got a strong voice, so she bolsters the choir's volume.

'Not sure how the vicar felt, though. From the little I've seen of him, I'd say Bob's a traditionalist, but he's very worried about keeping up numbers – so many churches are having to give up their choirs from lack of support. Perhaps he'd have welcomed Heather's decision. I'm not sure what he felt about the cremation, though.'

'What about the cremation?'

'Well, it happened straight after the service. The hearse took the coffin straight to the crematorium.'

'That's not unusual, is it?'

'I'd have thought it was unusual for the widow not to attend the cremation.'

'Happens quite often, I think,' said Jude. She had a friend who worked as a funeral celebrant and they had discussed such matters. 'You know, if she feels her duty is to be at the wake, to greet and talk to the guests, some of whom may have come a very long way to the funeral.'

'Maybe. Not sure how Bob would have felt about that. Maybe he would have welcomed it too. I don't know him well enough to be sure of his views. But I'm certain he didn't welcome the scene at the wake, though.'

'"Scene"?'

'There was a terrible set-to between Heather and her daughter.'

'Oh?'

'Well, I say "daughter". Stepdaughter, actually. Alice. You haven't . . . er . . .?'

'As I said, I haven't met any of them.'

'Anyway, the girl must have been drinking heavily. I can't understand how young people manage to drink so much. How anyone does, come to that. With me, alcohol wreaks absolute havoc with my IBS.'

Jude was reminded that, along with worries about his blood-sugar levels, Jonny Virgo was also troubled by Irritable Bowel Syndrome. And a few other Syndromes, too. In fact, she sometimes suspected that he only had to read the name of a Syndrome to develop it.

'But, apart from that,' he went on, 'I can never understand why people enjoy drinking too much. I've been on foreign trips with a choir I used to play for, and some of them . . . the amount they put away . . . it was frankly disgusting. The basses were always the worst, they were constantly having to be pulled out of bars. And other behaviour was pretty appalling too. You know, extramarital affairs going on. And none of them seemed to feel any guilt about it. They'd just giggle and say: "What happens on tour stays on tour." Which I don't think is a very responsible attitude.' There was quite a prudish side to Jonny Virgo.

'Could you just turn over?' asked Jude.

Jonny did as instructed and allowed her to start her ministrations to the front of his body. Still her hands didn't touch, just outlining his contours, feeling the tensions, easing the knots. He continued his narrative. 'So far as I could gather, there weren't meant to be any speeches in the church hall. Everything appropriate had been said in the church. But if that was the intention . . . well, Alice Mallett clearly hadn't got the message.'

'Oh?'

'It was most embarrassing. She was carrying an empty champagne bottle . . . and from the way she behaved, she might well have drunk all its contents . . . Anyway, she banged it on the table and announced that she wanted to say a few words. And dear oh dear, the "few words" she said were entirely inappropriate to the occasion.'

'In what way?'

'What she said was, basically, that her step-mother, Heather, had ruined her father's life. She implied that Heather had seduced him away from his first wife, which was totally untrue.'

'How do you know that, Jonny?'

'Because Heather and Leonard actually got married at All Saints, and I played the organ at their wedding. I remember it well, because I woke up that morning with a particularly bad migraine, and my mother said I should call in sick, but I said I couldn't let them down. So, I did play for them, though I was feeling pretty terrible throughout the whole ceremony. And I'd discussed with both Heather and Leonard what hymns they would have, and so I got to know the pair of them a bit. And Leonard told me that his first wife had died some ten years before, and he'd only known Heather for eight months.'

'So, Alice was lying?'

'Well . . . obviously.'

'Yes.' Jude was thoughtful. 'Of course, it is possible that they'd had a secret relationship before, which nobody else knew about, and Alice found out and—'

'No, Jude. Out of the question.'

'Oh?'

'You don't know Heather, do you?'

'No.'

'Well, she's the most prim and proper person you could ever meet. The idea of her having a secret relationship with a married man . . . it just wouldn't have happened.'

'If you say so. Which means that Alice *was* lying.'

'Must have been. But that wasn't all she said in the church hall this morning.' Jude didn't need to prompt Jonny further; he was caught up in the momentum of his narrative. 'She said that Heather had made her father's life a complete misery. Alice said she had only married him for his money – he was quite high up in the insurance world, you know. And Heather had made him change his will, so that she – Alice – was completely cut out of it. Then, as soon as the will had been changed, Heather had no further use for Leonard.'

'And what sort of state was Alice in while she said all this?'

'Drunk, like I said. And totally hysterical.'

'If she'd lied about her father having a relationship with Heather before her mother did, then the rest might all have been lies as well.'

'Oh, I agree. Alice is a most unreliable witness.'

'And do we know how Leonard Mallett actually died?'

'He had a fall, apparently. Fell downstairs.'

'And he was how old?'

'Late seventies, I'd say. Maybe early eighties.'

'So not an unlikely age for him to have had a fall.'

'No, certainly not. I do worry about something like that happening to me. It's an issue of balance, I think my internal gyroscope is not working quite as it should. I do sometimes feel very unsteady when I've been sitting somewhere for a long time, you know, at the piano or—'

Jude cut through the hypochondria. 'Do you know if the fall killed him, or if he died in hospital?'

'Oh, the fall did it. Apparently, Heather came back to the house, from wherever she'd been – shopping, I think – and found his body at the foot of the stairs.'

Jude didn't think it was the moment to comment that in most crime novels – and many real-life crime scenarios – the person who discovers the body is always the first suspect. Instead, she asked, 'What did Alice say this afternoon, about the actual death?'

'She said it wasn't an accident.'
'That he was pushed?'
'Yes.'
'The oldest question in crime – and in crime fiction, too: "Did he fall or was he pushed?"'
'That's the one.'
'And the pusher was presumably said to be Heather?'
'Oh yes. Alice said there was no doubt about it. Heather killed her husband for his money. It was definitely murder.'

Three

After Jonny had left, it was characteristic of Jude that she went straight round to High Tor to propose that, having turned down her neighbour's suggestion of going to the Crown & Anchor at lunchtime, they should go early evening instead. And it was characteristic of Carole that she hummed and hawed a great deal, as if evaluating other pressing demands on her time, before she agreed to go. And when Jude proposed they go at five, Carole felt a disapproving flutter at the thought of having a drink before the end of the working day (though it was some time since she last had a conventional working day, since she had retired from the Home Office).

At five, they walked together past the parade of shops to Fethering's only pub.

Ted Crisp, the landlord, was still dressed in his winter uniform of faded sweatshirt and grubby jeans, rather than his summer ensemble of faded T-shirt and grubby jeans. He greeted them with his customary gruffness. 'So, would I be jumping the gun to pour out two large New Zealand Sauvignon Blancs?'

'No,' Jude replied. 'You would be doing absolutely the right thing, and making us feel like regulars. Which is exactly what we like to think we are.'

'Good.' He looked at Carole. 'You know, I dreamt about you last night.'

'Did you?'

'No, you wouldn't let me.'

Jude giggled. Ted could never quite get away from his past as a stand-up comedian, though the quality of his jokes, as in this case, demonstrated why he never made a go of it.

Carole's reaction was more complex than her neighbour's. Though she understood the joke – which was not always the case with her and jokes – the innuendo couldn't fail to remind her of the unlikely truth that she and the landlord had once had a brief affair. She coloured and looked away.

Serendipitously, further conversation was interrupted by a burst of riotous laughter from the back of the pub near the French windows which, in the summer, were opened out on to the beach. Jude looked at her big round watch. 'A bit early for that kind of raucousness, isn't it?'

Ted tutted and raised his eyes to the heavens. 'That lot've been here all afternoon . . .'

'Then I think we'll sit up this end,' said Carole, whose entire life had been devoted to the avoidance of 'scenes'.

'They came on here from some post-funeral drinks do in the church hall,' he went on.

'Oh, I think we'll sit down there,' said Jude.

In the residual afternoon sunlight, Carole recognized all of the group sitting at a wooden table in the alcove as members of the church choir. The bearded Ruskin Dewitt and the thin-faced woman were there, along with a couple of ladies (definitely, in Fethering, 'ladies' rather than 'women') in their sixties. These Carole knew to be sisters, called Shirley and Veronica Tattersall, who lived together in a flat near the Fethering Yacht Club. She also knew the name of a tall, thin woman with unlikely long red hair. Elizabeth Browning, who only lacked the 'Barrett' to make herself the full Romantic Heroine. She was often to be seen, gliding soulfully along the streets of Fethering, like a lady from Chekhov who'd lost her lapdog. In fine weather during the summer, she frequently leaned against the stone wall which guarded the mouth of the River Fether, gazing soulfully out to sea, and generally doing an impression of the French Lieutenant's Woman.

Given that he'd shown no sign of recognizing her earlier in the day, Carole thought it unlikely that Ruskin Dewitt would suddenly remember who she was. She'd got the impression, from meeting him on the Preservation of Fethering's Seafront committee, that he lived in a bubble of his own pomposity and didn't notice other people much. Since she had never been introduced to the choir members whose names she did know, and since she didn't know the names of the others, she started towards a table as far away from them as possible.

But she hadn't reckoned with Jude's greater openness and conviviality. Inevitably, there was someone there who her neighbour knew.

It turned out to be Ruskin Dewitt. Of course. Men, Carole had convinced herself, were always suckers for Jude's rather obvious charms. He had risen immediately he saw her, disengaging himself clumsily from the fixed bench in the alcove. With a flamboyant gesture, he reached for her hand and planted a tickly kiss on to it. Not for the first time, Carole reflected on her low visibility when compared to that of her neighbour.

'Jude! My dear! What more could an old man ask than to have his afternoon animated by such a vision of pulchritude?'

'Nice to see you, Russ.' Whatever destination she'd had in mind, Carole was hauled back towards the group. 'Russ, I don't think you know my neighbour, Carole.'

'I don't believe I do. Though I have to say, young lady, that you do look familiar.'

Carole winced, as she always did at compliments.

'She was at the funeral,' said the sharp-faced woman. 'And briefly in the church hall afterwards.'

'Oh, that's where I recognize you from, of course. Carole, was it?'

'That's right.' The words contained the frostiness with which she greeted all new acquaintances.

'My name is Ruskin Dewitt,' he said. (She was right. He'd completely forgotten that the two of them had ever sat on a committee together.) 'Citizen not of this parish, but of Fedborough, a little further up the River Fether. Formerly a purveyor of education in English Literature to young persons who were unaware of the privilege they were receiving by being taught by me. But, Carole, you will join us?'

'Erm . . . Well . . .'

'Of course we will,' said Jude. She looked at the table. There were some glasses with dregs of wine in them, and a bottle of white so deep into an ice bucket that it was impossible to see whether it was full or empty. 'Are you all right for drinks?'

'I think we're fine, Jude my angel,' said Ruskin Dewitt, unsteadily reinserting himself into his seat. 'We were actually talking about leaving.'

'We've been talking about leaving all afternoon,' said the thin-faced woman. She looked at her watch. 'I should be getting back for Rory.'

But none of them made any move. Further introductions were made. The names of the older women, Shirley and Veronica Tattersall, were vaguely familiar to Carole and Jude. They were also introduced to the self-appointed Tragedy Queen of Fethering, Elizabeth Browning. 'Of course, I have seen you both around,' she trilled, before embarking on an unrequested autobiography. 'I feel it's my duty to sing with the church choir. I was professional, you know, Glyndebourne way back, but . . .' She brought a hand up to her papery neck '. . . the nodules.'

'Ah,' said Jude.

'Cut my career short at a terribly early age.'

'I'm so sorry.'

Elizabeth Browning left a tragic pause, too long to prevent the younger woman from muscling in and introducing herself as Bet Harrison. 'Only moved down here a couple of weeks ago,' she said, providing the instant explanation of why they hadn't recognized her.

'You didn't take long to get into the choir,' said Jude.

'The church community is welcoming wherever you go.' Somehow Bet managed to avoid making her words sound sanctimonious.

'And we're always glad of new voices adding their strength to ours,' said Ruskin. 'Bob's particularly pleased. He gets very worried about dwindling numbers.'

This echo of Jonny Virgo's words made Jude suspect that the size of the All Saints choir was a real issue for the vicar. Perhaps he saw in it a reflection of declining attendance in the main body of the church. And maybe a reflection on his own competence.

'And it is good,' Bet went on, 'to know when you go to a new place, there'll be a church, where you can quickly find a group of like-minded people.'

Carole shuddered inwardly at the idea. She thought, for herself, the prospect of finding 'like-minded people' anywhere was pretty distant. She treasured her anonymity and exclusivity. When she'd moved permanently to Fethering, raw after her divorce and premature retirement from the Home Office, she hadn't wanted to make contact with anyone. She'd only bought Gulliver because she didn't wish to appear lonely when she walked on the beach. And if she'd had a neighbour with a less outgoing and persistent personality than Jude, that relationship wouldn't have flourished either.

'Of course, normally you'd hope to make friends at the school gate, too,' Bet went on. Jude was beginning to wonder whether she was usually this forthcoming, or if the drink had relaxed her. 'But my son Rory goes to the comprehensive in Clincham, so he gets a bus there and back. It's been difficult for him starting there in the middle of term, but that's just down to the logistics of when we could move. The English system of house purchase doesn't take notice of details like school terms.'

'Have you moved down from London?' asked Jude. Most of the people who ended up in Fethering had.

'No. Evesham. That's where Rory was born and brought up, but then my marriage broke down and . . . well, I wanted to get as far away from the place as possible. But, you know, house purchase . . . you think you've got somewhere sorted, then the chain breaks down, and . . . quite frankly, it's been a nightmare.'

Carole was beginning to think that they were being granted too much information. Was the woman going to provide her entire life story within minutes of meeting complete strangers? Was she equally revealing with everyone she met? Such behaviour went against Carole's every instinct.

Fortunately, at this moment Ruskin Dewitt re-entered the conversation. 'Did you know Leonard Mallett well, Carole?' he asked.

'Hardly at all.' And she mentioned the Preservation of Fethering's Seafront committee.

'Yes, well, I'm on that.' He screwed up his eyes and inspected her. 'Oh, I do recognize you now.'

'Good,' said Carole, with some acidity.

'And were you at the church hall earlier in the afternoon when things got rather ugly?'

'I heard Alice Mallett having a bit of a go at her step-mother.'

'"Having a bit of a go"? You have an enviable talent for understatement, Carole.'

'Yes, being new to the area,' said Bet, 'I was quite shocked. Are accusations of murder common events in Fethering?'

The group laughed at the idea. Carole and Jude exchanged covert looks. Each knew that accusations of murder had featured rather more in their lives than they had in that of the average village resident.

Elizabeth Browning, who hadn't joined in the communal laughter, said gnomically, 'Tragedies are not unknown in the village.' But the other choir members had heard her narratives too often to invite further explanation.

'Does anyone actually *know* anything about the circumstances of Leonard Mallett's death?' asked Carole. 'We've heard that he "had a fall", but that's it.'

Shirley and Veronica Tattersall regretted that they couldn't provide any more detail, but inevitably Ruskin Dewitt did have a contribution to make. 'I don't want to be telling tales out of school, and let me tell you, having spent most of my professional life in schools, I'm fully aware of the meaning of that expression . . . but I did hear something which might have some bearing on the subject of Leonard Mallett's death.'

'What was it?' demanded Carole, irritated at the orotundity of his narrative manner, and wanting to hurry him along a bit.

He looked a little piqued, as he said, 'Very well. A couple of months ago, on a Friday . . . you know, usual choir rehearsal night . . . Heather had a problem with her car. Should have been back from the garage late afternoon, but there was a part they couldn't get till the Saturday morning, something like that. So, since I come from Fedborough and virtually drive past the Shorelands Estate, I had a call from her asking if I could pick her up for rehearsal. No problem for me, and I have to confess I was rather intrigued. You know, Heather kept herself so much to herself, and I thought I might get the opportunity, on the car journey, which was only ten minutes, but I thought I might find out a little more about her, get to know her a bit. In a way, though, perhaps I got more than I bargained for.'

He took another suspenseful pause. Carole had great difficulty in stopping herself from telling him to get on with it.

'I knocked at the door, expecting Heather to come scuttling out, but it was opened by Leonard. I mean, I knew who he was, I'd seen him around the village, but I wouldn't say I *knew* him.

'Anyway, he wasn't particularly gracious to me . . . In fact, that's putting it mildly. He was damned rude – pardon my French. He said, "Oh, you've come to take her off for her bloody choir, have you?" And then he called off into the house, "For Christ's sake, Heather, your lift's arrived. What are you faffing around at? No amount of titivation is going to make you look any better at your age." Which I have to say is not the way that I was brought up to speak to a lady.'

'Did Heather say anything back to him,' asked Jude, 'you know, when she came to the door?'

'No, she seemed to be completely cowed. Shrank away when she passed him on her way out.'

Carole was immediately aware of the contrast with the cheerful woman she had seen drinking in the church hall. The woman with new glasses, the woman who'd let her hair grow.

'And did Leonard have any parting shot for her?' asked Jude.

'Yes. He said, "Off you go to church then. Maybe God can help sort you out. He's supposed to have a decent record with lost causes, isn't he?" I remember the words exactly, because . . . well, because I don't think I've ever heard a husband be so rude to his wife.'

'Makes you understand the level of relief she must have felt . . .' said Carole, 'you know, when he was no longer on the scene. It must've been absolutely ghastly for her, the whole marriage.'

'You never know,' said Jude, who had had a lot of marital secrets shared from her treatment couch. 'It may have been what worked for them, what turned them on. You can never look inside another marriage.'

'I agree.' Carole had certainly never wanted anyone looking inside her marriage to David. Or their divorce, come to that. 'But the way Heather was behaving in the church hall suggested someone who had just had a great burden lifted off her shoulders.'

'And the way she was behaving here,' Bet Harrison contributed.

'She was here?' asked Carole, surprised.

Ruskin Dewitt nodded vigorously, setting a ripple through the foliage of his beard. 'Yes. As I was leaving the church hall, I said, sort of casually, that some of the choir were going to the Crown & Anchor for a drink, and Heather said, to my amazement, "See you there!" She only left half an hour ago.'

'Goodness.' Carole and Jude exchanged a look, both regretting that they hadn't joined the party earlier. Carole looked at her watch. Nearly six. Say formalities in the church hall had finished round two thirty, the session in the pub had been going on for a good three hours. And, until recently, the bereaved widow had been part of it.

'Incidentally,' said Carole, drawing Ruskin Dewitt back to his earlier conversation, 'did Heather say anything to you in the car on the way to rehearsal, you know, that day, after her husband had been so rude to her?'

'I didn't think she was going to. And I didn't really think it was my place to make any comment, but after a long silence, when we were nearly at the church, Heather did apologize for her husband's behaviour. She said, "He gets like that. I'm afraid Leonard hasn't taken very well to retirement." Something of an understatement, I thought, but I just mumbled a few words about it being very difficult for her. And she said – and goodness, I don't think I'll ever forget her words . . .'

On this occasion, Carole did not allow him to

indulge in his full dramatic pause. 'What did she say?' she asked testily.

'Heather said,' Ruskin replied, '"Oh, he'll get his comeuppance. There's nothing so deadly as a worm that's turned."'

Four

The other drinkers melted away into the late afternoon. Carole and Jude found themselves alone with Bet Harrison. They noticed, when Jude went to get more Sauvignon Blanc, that she was only drinking mineral water (so it hadn't been alcohol that made her so forthcoming, it was her normal manner). 'And thanks,' she said, when offered a top-up, 'but I don't need any more.'

'Bit of a bugger,' she went on to Carole while Jude was at the bar, 'not drinking on an occasion like this, but Rory needs ferrying somewhere this evening. I'm stuck in the driving years, which seem to be going on for ever, and without having a partner to share the burden, I daren't risk losing my licence, particularly living down here and . . . well . . . Do you have children?'

Though this was, by her standards, a rather over-direct question, Carole could not deny that she had a son Stephen, who was married with two daughters. It was not in her nature to mention to a new acquaintance how much joy her grandchildren had brought into her life.

'Ah, well, you must have done the driving years bit, too.'

'Yes, but we were living in London back then, so it probably wasn't so bad. Stephen could go most places on public transport.'

'Right. What does your husband do?'

'I'm divorced,' said Carole, in a tone which she hoped would deter further enquiry.

It failed. 'Join the club,' said Bet. 'Though if I was still married, I wouldn't be getting much help with ferrying Rory around. Waste of space, my husband was, when it came to anything practical. Great skill men have, avoiding responsibility, don't they? Even in this day and age—'

Fortunately, the arrival of Jude with two large Sauvignon Blancs stemmed the feminist flow. 'Just talking about children,' said Bet.

'Ah. I don't have any.' Jude was always very easy about getting that bit of information into a conversation. When they first met, Carole thought her neighbour must feel some level of sadness about her childlessness, but now she had come round to the view that it genuinely didn't worry her. Jude had always been better than Carole at accepting the hand life had dealt her. And, perhaps as a result, in Carole's view her neighbour always seemed to have better cards.

'Well,' said Bet, 'that means you're missing out on the dubious pleasure of being a glorified taxi service.' She looked suddenly at Jude. 'Incidentally, I know you weren't at the funeral – or the church hall – but do you know Heather Mallett?' A shake of the head by way of response. 'I was just interested in what Russ was saying, you know, about when he gave her the lift. Sounds like she was stuck in a really abusive marriage.'

'Hard to be sure without knowing more detail,' said Jude diplomatically. 'Verbal abuse doesn't definitely mean there's also physical abuse. Some couples just are combative. They seem to get off on it.'

'Well, he was combative, we know that. Doesn't sound like Heather did much in the way of getting back at him.'

'Who can say?'

'Unless, of course, she actually did help him on his way down those stairs.'

'We have no means of knowing—'

'If she did,' Bet interrupted, 'I'd say good for her. Women have been victims of male aggression for far too long. Do you know, it wasn't until the 1878 Matrimonial Causes Act that women in this country could seek legal separation from an abusive husband. Up until then they were just chattels. It's amazing how today's women suffer from that legacy of discrimination. And there are still . . .'

Maybe it was Carole's discreet throat-clearing that got her down off her soapbox, or just a glance at her watch. 'God! I must go. Get back to Rory. I've left him on his own for quite long enough.'

'He's not at school?' asked Jude.

'No, I got him out for the funeral.'

'But surely he didn't know Leonard Mallett?'

'No, no, of course he didn't. Oh, you weren't there, so you wouldn't have seen him. Rory sings in the church choir with me, and I thought it was better for him to miss a day's school and get some social interaction locally.' She giggled guiltily. 'I just said to the school that he had to go to a funeral, and they assumed it must've been someone close, so there were no problems about it. I took the day off, too.' She took another look at her watch. 'And now my small window of freedom is about to close again.'

'Where do you work?' asked Carole.

The thin face grimaced. 'Starbucks on the Parade.'

'Oh?' This was another of Carole's deeply layered monosyllables. She didn't approve of Starbucks, or any other international chain. She had preferred it when the café on the Parade had been Polly's Cake Shop. She was generally suspicious of change.

Possibly prompted by Carole's disapproval, Bet felt the need to apologize for her job. 'It's only temporary, until I get something better, but it's difficult in a place like this. The trouble is, I got married too young, you know, before I had any qualifications. It didn't seem important at the time, but back then, of course, I thought the marriage was going to be for life. It didn't occur to me that my bastard husband . . .'

Maybe she caught the exasperated look that Carole flicked at Jude, or maybe she just recollected that she was up against time, but Bet Harrison stopped herself there. She made a big deal of saying how much she'd enjoyed meeting them, and how much she looked forward to seeing them again.

'Huh,' said Carole, when the woman was out of earshot. 'I do resent people who feel that they have to spill out their entire life history the moment you meet them.'

Jude knew this was just one of many things her neighbour resented, but all she said, very casually, was, 'She's just lonely. Coming to a new place, not knowing anyone, she's only trying to make contact.'

'Well,' said Carole beadily, 'you've always had a more generous view of humanity than I have.'

This was so self-evidently true as to require no comment.

As they walked through the interior of the pub, it was still fairly empty. Ted Crisp often bemoaned the fact that there were fewer casual drinkers than there used to be. 'Never been the same since breathalyser came in,' he frequently stated. 'Lovely girl, Breath Eliza, she had this way of blowing in your ear, you know,' he always added, demonstrating once again why his career in stand-up had struggled to get off the ground.

Perhaps one of the reasons for the dearth of casual drinkers was that the identity of the Crown & Anchor had changed since Ted engaged a chef called Ed Pollack, whose cooking had raised the profile of the pub's restaurant considerably. In fact, the place was now frequently referred to – in an expression the landlord loathed – as a 'gastropub'. In its new incarnation, booking was essential, and the busy time had shifted from early evening to dinner. A lot of the local drinkers felt it was no longer the place for a quiet pint.

With Ed in the kitchen, and the bars under the expert management of the pigtailed Polish Zosia, the Crown & Anchor had undoubtedly become 'a success'. But Ted Crisp didn't let a detail like that alter his customary lugubrious demeanour. And he would never let the pub's gentrification affect his wardrobe choices.

As Carole and Jude passed, he was leaning over the bar, talking to a fiftyish man, whose thinning hair was pulled back into a sparse ponytail. The man wore a pale denim jacket, shirt and jeans, clasped with a broad brown leather belt, and scuffed cowboy boots. There was a half-empty pint glass of Guinness in front of him.

'Ah. Carole,' said Ted, 'I don't think you've met . . .'

'Hello, KK,' said Jude.

A little tug of annoyance pulled at Carole's lower lip. This happened far too often in Fethering, she thought, Jude knowing more people than she did. And Carole had lived there longer. Registering the man's scruffiness, she reckoned he must be one of the flaky types her neighbour had met through the healing practice.

'Hi, Jude.' He got off his bar stool and enveloped her in a huge hug.

'Good to see you.' The hug was returned with reciprocal warmth. Carole's first thought was that this must be another of Jude's lovers. There had certainly been a good few of them (though not nearly as many as there were in Carole's imagination).

When she had disengaged herself from the bear hug, Jude said, 'This is Carole, my neighbour.'

'Hi.' The denim-clad creature extended the monosyllable into something long and languid.

'Oh, I thought you'd know each other,' said Ted.

'No, said Carole frostily.

'KK's a musician,' said Jude.

'Ah,' said Carole, as if that explained everything.

'"A wandering minstrel, I . . ."' The words,

spoken rather than sung, were a surprise. KK's image was more Bruce Springsteen than Gilbert & Sullivan.

Ted Crisp picked up his cue, 'Available for every kind of function – birthdays, christenings, bar mitzvahs, weddings, divorces . . . You name it, KK's up for the gig.'

'Yeah,' the musician agreed. 'Up for anything that pays the bills . . . Though there's not much work around at the minute.'

'Never is, is there?' Ted sympathized, perhaps thinking back to his stand-up days.

'I'm based in Worthing,' KK went on, 'and I used to do a lot of gigs round all the pubs in the area, into Hampshire, Kent even. My band's called Rubber Truncheon.' He paused for a nano-second, like all performers do, but receiving no flicker of name recognition, went on, 'I used to do regular gigs here, didn't I, Ted?'

'Yeah, all right, don't go on about it.'

'I mean, Monday evenings, they're always quiet. Hardly worth you opening up then. But, like I've said before, if you had a bit of live music, that'd bring the punters in, always has done. Then they get loyal to the band and you find you've built up a fan-base in no time. Bit of social media coverage, lots of bands have got relaunched that way. And, of course, the pub that's their venue, they benefit from it, and all. Sales of booze go up. I'm sure, Ted, if you tried, you could—'

'I've told you a thousand times, KK. It's not my fault. Government changed the laws, didn't they? Got to have a licence for music now. Made it too expensive to have the live stuff. Days of a couple of blokes with guitars strumming away in the corner, they're long gone.'

'You could afford it, Ted,' said the musician. 'Now your restaurant's in all those guides and everything, you must be sitting on a little goldmine here.'

'Whether that's true or not – and actually it's not – I'm still not convinced that my restaurant guests want to be serenaded by the music of Rubber Truncheon.'

'There's nothing wrong with my music!'

The landlord backed down quickly. 'I didn't say there was, KK. And it's not your music I'm objecting to. Will you get it into your head – it's nothing personal, it's the price of a bloody music licence!'

Carole looked at Jude, trying to indicate with her eyebrows that there was really no need for them to be further involved in this exchange. But, infuriatingly, Jude indicated with a slight head movement that she wanted to stay. Even more infuriatingly, she said, 'I think perhaps we'd better have another drink, Ted.'

Three large Sauvignon Blancs so early in the evening did not accord with Carole's proprieties. But then again, if she said no, or asked for a mineral water, or went home on her own, that would definitely look like a snub to Jude. It was yet another social quandary. To her surprise, her lips formed the words, 'I'll get these. It's my turn.'

So, a few minutes later, she found herself sitting down in an alcove with Jude and KK.

Annoyingly, though the light way the two talked suggested they knew each other well, they gave no indication of how they had met, or how long ago. Nor did they give any indication of the level of intimacy at which their friendship had been conducted. And there was no way Carole was going to *ask*.

Despite his uncouth appearance, KK seemed to have been well brought up. His laid-back vowels occasionally slipped into something which might have been the product of private education. And he was conscious that Carole shouldn't be left out of the conversation. After giving Jude an update on the doings of a drummer called Miff who they apparently both knew, and who KK had been working with in Holland until a few days previously, he turned the considerable charm of his smile on to her neighbour.

'You're looking very smart, Carole, for a visit down to the old C & A. Have you come straight from work?'

'I'm retired,' she replied awkwardly. 'I was actually at a funeral this morning.'

'Oh?' KK's face took on a suitably compassionate expression. 'I hope it wasn't someone close.'

'No, no. I hardly knew him. Just someone from the village.'

'Anyone I'd know?'

'I very much doubt it.' Carole doubted that the two men would have had much in common. 'Man called Leonard Mallett.'

The effect her words had on KK was a total surprise. He looked as if he'd been hit by a lead-filled sock. He managed to gasp out the question, 'How did he die?'

'Fell down the stairs.'

'My God.' The musician shook his head slowly. 'So, Heather finally did it.'

Five

Carole tried to get KK to expand on what he'd just said, but before she'd finished the question, he'd downed the remains of his Guinness, said he had to go to rehearse for a gig, and left the pub.

'That's strange,' Ted Crisp observed. 'For a start, KK prides himself on never rehearsing. And, what's more, he hasn't got any gigs.'

'Now I know that neither of you are regular church-goers . . .'

'Not any kind of church-goers,' said Carole tartly. The vicar had arrived at High Tor when Jude was there for coffee, and since he said he was there simply for a 'pastoral visit', there was a logic to his speaking to both women at the same time.

'Well, I saw you at Leonard Mallett's funeral yesterday,' he pointed out.

'Attending funerals is hardly "regular church-going". It's simply obeying a social convention.'

'Perhaps. But it is always my hope that people attending All Saints, for whatever reason, may begin to understand what the church is there for. I think a lot of the anti-church sentiment around is based on ignorance of what actually happens inside churches.'

'Quite possibly,' said Jude, always more emollient than her neighbour.

The new vicar of All Saints was a short, earnest man with thick glasses. He didn't wear a dog collar, except when he was conducting services, probably feeling that jeans and a polo shirt made him look more approachable. He didn't look like a man with much sense of humour.

'Anyway,' Jude went on. 'I'm certainly not "anti-church". I think churches have done a lot of good for society over the years – and are still doing it, particularly now government support for local services is so diminished. I've often put my clients – I'm a healer, incidentally – in touch with facilities run by local churches. So I've nothing against churches, *per se*. All I lack is that essential ingredient, which might persuade me I need to go to church every week. In other words, faith.'

'Faith may come,' said the vicar. 'Never rule it out. It came to me in a most unexpected way.'

'Really?' said Carole, in a way that she hoped would deter him from telling them all the details.

Fortunately, he moved on. 'I said I'd come on a "pastoral visit", and that is certainly true. Everything that happens in the parish is of concern to me. But there is one specific subject that I wanted to raise with you . . .'

Carole produced a slightly less deterrent 'Oh?'

'Did you go to the church hall after the funeral yesterday?'

'I did. Briefly.'

'Were you there to witness the scene between Alice Mallett and her stepmother?'

'I saw the beginning of it, yes.'

'I was very shocked by what happened.'

'I can see that it's not the kind of behaviour that's expected at funerals.'

'Certainly not. Obviously, I'm very new to Fethering, Carole, but I wondered if you knew whether there was a history of bad blood between mother and stepdaughter?'

'Local gossip says they don't get along.'

'And what is that based on?'

Carole shrugged. 'Probably nothing. Like the majority of local gossip.'

'That scene in the church hall really troubled me.' The vicar did look genuinely distressed. 'I mean, I see it as my duty to heal rifts in the relationships of my parishioners. Bringing them the message of Christianity. Being, as St Francis put it, "an instrument" of God's peace. I see that as part of my job. In fact, that's how I would define "pastoral care".'

'It's an admirable ambition,' said Jude gently, 'but you're going to have your work cut out if you want to heal all of the relationship rifts in Fethering.'

'I know, but since this recent confrontation took place on church premises . . . well, I do feel I have to find out as much as I can about it . . . you know, see if I can improve things.'

Carole and Jude exchanged sceptical looks.

'I have to try,' the vicar asserted. 'It was an accusation of murder.' They still didn't look convinced. 'And with the police being involved . . .'

Now he had their attention. 'How are the police

involved?' asked Carole. 'Did someone who'd been in the church hall contact them?'

'No, I think they'd been tipped the wink before that. They implied allegations had been made some time earlier in the week.'

'What allegations?'

'That Heather Mallett had had a hand in her husband's death.'

'When did they say this?' asked Jude. 'Have they spoken to you?'

'Yes. Two plainclothesmen came round to the vicarage this morning.'

'And what did you find out from them?' asked Carole. 'Did they talk in terms of murder?'

'No. I think police probably avoid that word as much as they can. Until they have proof, anyway. They said they had an anonymous tip-off on Wednesday, from a woman in a public phone box.'

'Not so many of those around these days,' observed Jude. 'Public phone boxes, that is. Everyone uses mobiles.'

'But there are some. If you can find one, and ensure there are no witnesses around, it remains a fairly efficient way of maintaining your anonymity.'

'So, did the police reckon the accusation came from Alice Mallett?'

'If they did think so, they didn't share the information with me.' The vicar sounded a little put out.

'No, police are rotten like that, aren't they?' said Jude, with feeling.

'Did they mention whether they had spoken to Alice?'

'No, but I got the impression that was on their list of things to do. They were talking to me as an eyewitness to what actually happened in the church hall; you know, to get some background details. I don't know that I was that much help to them on that, having arrived in Fethering so relatively recently. I hardly know the Malletts.'

'Nor does anyone else, really,' said Jude.

'Do you know if the police have spoken to Heather?' asked Carole.

'They didn't actually say so, but I got the impression, from something they said, that they were going to see her when they'd finished talking to me.'

'And did you also get the impression they might want to talk to you again?'

'They said it was a possibility but didn't make it sound very likely. It seemed to me that they didn't really take the supposed crime seriously, they were just going through the motions.'

'What makes you say that?' asked Carole, her Home Office antennae alerted.

'Well, if they did think there was much substance in the accusation, they'd have stopped the funeral, wouldn't they? Certainly have stopped the cremation?'

'You're right.'

'But all they did when they left was ask me to contact them if I heard anything else that might be relevant. And they advised me to talk as little about the situation as possible.'

In response to Carole's quizzical look, the vicar said, 'All right, that's exactly what I'm doing, I know. But I'm doing it because of my job. I feel it's part of my remit here in Fethering to create as much harmony as possible. What I witnessed in the church hall yesterday distressed me very much. If I could effect a rapprochement between Heather Mallett and her stepdaughter . . . well, I'd feel that was the kind of pastoral role I should be taking on. That's what I'm here for.'

He spoke with idealistic earnestness. Jude found herself wondering what kind of a man he had been before his 'Damascene conversion'. Had finding God actually changed his character, or had he always had the same humourless focus, but directed it towards other goals?

'I think that sounds very admirable,' she said, hoping the words didn't sound patronizing.

But Bob Hinkley was too busy riding his hobby-horse to worry about any such nuance. 'I really do feel I've been chosen with a view to making the church relevant, showing people why it should be at the centre of their lives, rather than on the periphery. And because I had a life in the commercial world before I was ordained, I feel I can perhaps bring more practical skills to the task than, say, someone whose whole career has been in the church. I believe that, in this age of rampant commercialism, cyber-bullying and fake news, the church has never been more relevant. And what I'm talking about is a very broad church, that embraces everyone, regardless of gender, race or sexual orientation.'

He was looking straight at Jude as he said this, and she knew exactly what he meant. It wasn't the first time that the closeness of the two neigh-bours had been interpreted as something rather more meaningful. In fact, she knew that a small constituency of Fethering residents were absolutely convinced they were a lesbian couple. Fortunately, though, Carole, out of his eye-line, hadn't picked up the vicar's implication. She hadn't picked up the lesbian subtext, which was just as well. Carole always got deeply offended by such suggestions, whereas Jude thought they were very funny.

'Anyway,' Bob Hinkley went on, 'while I'm here, there is something else I wanted to talk about.'

'Oh?'

'The choir.'

'What about the choir?' said Carole. Then, feeling that might have sounded a bit graceless, she added, 'They were in good voice yesterday.'

'Yes, they were. I think the organist, Jonny Virgo . . .'

'I know him,' said Jude, with no mention of the context.

'Ah. Well, I think he has his work cut out with them. Some of the voices are not quite as . . . well . . . You can always hear when someone's flat, can't you? Not of course that I don't appreciate the time and effort that the people put into it. Hm, anyway, with the choir . . . and indeed, with the congregation . . . I am aware that the average age of the participants is high and that, not to put too fine a point on it, numbers are dwindling.'

'It's a trend that's happening across the country,' Jude sympathized.

'I know, but it's a trend that I feel it is in my remit to reverse.'

Carole, who was wondering if his second use of the word 'remit' was a hangover from his days 'in industry', murmured, 'Good luck.'

'So, I'm very actively trying to recruit new members.'

Jude spread her hands wide in apology. 'I'm sorry, but as we've said, we both lack the faith that makes church attendance seem necessary to us.'

'I wasn't talking about the congregation. I was talking about the choir.'

'What, you're trying to enlist non-believers into the church choir?' asked Carole.

'I'm trying to enlist *anyone* into the church choir.' The pleading in Bob Hinkley's voice was a measure of his desperation. Both women realized how much he was investing in his new career, the high goals that he had set himself. If he was on a one-man mission to reverse the rising tide of godlessness in the country, they feared he was lining himself up for disappointment.

'I don't sing,' said Carole definitively.

'You mean you can't sing?'

'Yes.' But she wasn't sure if the answer was true. Like many of Carole's inhibitions, this one went back a long way. When she started, aged thirteen, at her private girl's school, the music mistress had asked each member of the class to stand up and sing, to assess their suitability for the school choir. Carole had found this exposure so acutely nerve-wracking that, from that moment on, she had never let a musical sound come out of her mouth. At assemblies and church services she had become very expert at lip-synching and sounding final consonants, so that she looked as if she was singing. But she allowed no actual noise to emerge.

And from that time on, if ever the subject came up, she insisted that she couldn't sing. There was nothing less appealing to Carole Seddon than standing up in front of people and being asked to entertain them. Though, as she had often proved in her Home Office days, she was more than competent at chairing difficult meetings, the idea of public performance was anathema to her.

In reflective moods, she did sometimes wonder whether there was innate music in her, which had been frightened away by the music mistress's demands. There were some songs she liked, some tunes that she found soothing. And she had often found herself singing nursery rhymes to her grandchildren, Lily and Chloe (when she was sure their parents were not within earshot). The little girls had never made any objections.

But a direct question, like the one that had just been posed by the Rev. Bob Hinkley, would always still receive the steely reply that she couldn't sing.

'What about you, Jude?' he asked.

'Well, I can sing all right . . .' Yes, of course she'd be able to, thought Carole bitterly. Singing involved being relaxed, and Jude was good at that. She'd been an actress at some stage in her life, too. That must've involved singing.

'But,' her friend went on, 'I don't really want to commit myself to—'

She was interrupted by a ringing from the vicar's

phone. 'Excuse me.' He looked at the display. 'I'd better take this. It's the police.'

During the call, Carole and Jude exchanged looks of frustration. Most of Bob's responses were 'Yes' or 'Right'. It was impossible to guess what information he was responding to.

When he ended the call, they both looked at him expectantly.

'Well?' demanded Carole. 'Is there anything you can tell us?'

'Yes, there is,' he replied slowly. 'In fact, they want me to tell you. They want everyone in Fethering to get the message. So, as they put it, all of the gossip and accusations will stop.'

'What is the message they want everyone to get?'

'That the police are concluding their investigations. They are convinced there was nothing suspicious about the fall that killed Leonard Mallett. He died a natural death.'

Six

Within a week, the ripples caused by the scene at Leonard Mallett's wake had spread outwards to nothingness, and the placid, level surface of Fethering life returned. A new report on the possible rerouting of the A27 around Fedborough (an issue which had been reported on every three years for the past thirty without ever prompting any action) provided fresh material for argument among the sages at the bar of the Crown & Anchor. And Fethering gossip continued to create elaborate fabrications, into whose weave were inserted a few narrow threads of truth.

Only Carole and Jude, it seemed, regarded investigation into the circumstances of Leonard Mallett's death as unfinished business. And, with the passage of time, even their urgency to do something faded.

'No, what I'm talking about is a community choir,' said Heather Mallett.

'Based here in the pub?' asked Ted Crisp.

'Yes, exactly,' said KK Rosser.

Carole and Jude were pleased to be part of the little group in the Crown & Anchor that Wednesday evening. Though Jude would not have stood on ceremony, Carole felt reassured that their previous introduction to KK, by the arcane protocols of Fethering, justified their being introduced to Heather Mallett, a woman who still held an aura of mystery for her.

Now it wasn't just the glasses and the longer hair that had transformed her previously beige image. The glasses were there, the oxblood ones she had worn at the funeral. And the hair had now been skilfully shaped and animated with a bit of bottled colour. But the rest of her wardrobe had changed too. It was now late March, and unseasonally warm enough for Fethering residents to murmur darkly about global warming. To match the weather, Heather Mallett was dressed in a linen shirt with vertical blue and white stripes over scarlet linen trousers. On her feet were white canvas espadrilles.

Her manner had changed too. Of course, neither Carole nor Jude had ever spent time with her before, but they had heard reports around the village of her generally cowed demeanour. It was certainly unexpected to see her being so expansive in the Crown & Anchor and taking the initiative with Ted Crisp.

'So, let me get this straight,' said the landlord. 'The idea is that you run the choir here . . . what, once a month?'

'No, once a week,' Heather replied.

'Yes,' KK agreed. 'Mondays. Like you're always saying, business is slack on Mondays.'

'And what about me having to get an entertainment licence?'

'No problem. The choir wouldn't be entertaining people.'

'Oh, you're going to be that bad, are you?' asked the landlord, and guffawed.

'Ha bloody ha.' The guitarist grinned wearily. 'I do set them up for you, don't I, Ted?'

'Yeah. Very generous, thanks.'

'No, but the point is,' KK went on, 'that we'd just be rehearsing here, like for fun.'

'Sorry, I don't get it.'

Heather intervened. 'The fact is, Ted, that a lot of people like singing with a choir, just for the sake of it.'

'Do they?'

'It's an extremely popular leisure activity. Very therapeutic, too.'

'I've heard that.' The landlord shook his shaggy head. 'I must say I don't get it. Being in a choir with all them other people. If I'm on stage – you know, like back when I was doing the stand-up – I want people looking at me. God, if I'm putting in all that effort, I want people to know what I'm doing. Don't see the fun of being with a group, where nobody notices whether you're there or not.'

'No,' Heather agreed, 'you don't get it, do you? But there are people out there, you know, who get a real charge from community activities.'

'Well, I don't.' Carole couldn't stop herself. She'd always considered that attaching the prefix 'community' to any activity was the kiss of death, and had only just stopped herself from speaking the first time Heather used the word.

'That's fair enough.' The widow smiled. 'No one's going to force anyone to be part of the choir. There'll be no three-line whip. It would only be for people who wanted to take part.'

'And how would you find those people? Put ads in the Post Office window?'

'Probably be more effective to put something in the village online newsletter.'

'Oh?' Carole was aware that such a thing existed, though there was no danger of her ever subscribing to it.

'Yes, that can be very effective,' said Jude. Typical of her not to show solidarity, thought her neighbour sniffily. 'I've got quite a few clients that way.' Something else Carole didn't know.

'So, what do you say, Ted?' Heather turned her brown eyes on him appealingly, almost flirtatiously. 'Will you let us give it a go?'

'Well . . .'

'Come on,' said KK. 'You know Monday nights are dead for business. If people come in for the choir, they're going to buy drinks, aren't they?'

'Maybe. Things pick up, though, once you get to May and June.'

'All right, well, just let us try once, in the next couple of weeks. See who comes along.'

Ted Crisp was on the way to being persuaded. 'So how would it work?'

Heather took over. She and KK had clearly thought the whole thing through. 'We'd meet early evening, half past six, seven . . .'

Ted looked round the bar. 'Where?'

'In the Function Room.'

'And do I get paid normal rates for the use of the Function Room?'

'No, of course you don't,' replied Heather, almost winsomely. 'You let us use it for free.'

'And why would I do that?'

'Out of the goodness of your heart.'
'Huh. How d'you know there's any goodness in there?'
'You also do it,' said KK, 'because of all the drinks the choir members are going to buy.'
'Oh yeah? I'll believe that when it happens. Anyway, what kind of music will it be? I don't want hymns and that driving out the few customers I do get. Nothing like "O God Our Help in Ages Past" for putting a damper on an evening.'
'It won't be hymns,' said Heather. 'It'll be more, sort of, light popular stuff.'
'Kind of songs I play,' KK added.
'Bloody hell, that's all we need!' But Ted grinned as he said it. 'And may I ask what your role in the proceedings will be?'
Heather provided the answer for him. 'KK would be the choirmaster.'
'That sounds a bit posh to me,' the musician objected. 'A bit po-faced and churchy. But yeah, I'd be, like, the one who leads the sessions, you know, playing the music, showing them how to do the harmonies, that stuff.'
'Hmm . . .' Ted Crisp sounded uncertain.
'I've done this kind of thing before. In a pub in Brighton. Went very well.'
'If it went very well back in Brighton, why aren't you still doing it there?'
'It was . . . um . . .' KK looked uncomfortable. 'It didn't work out. Artistic differences.'
'Oh yeah? And, incidentally, what's in it for you?'
'Sorry?'
'Money, KK, money. Because if you think I'm

going to pay you, as well as giving you use of the Function Room for free, then you've got another—'

'No, no, you wouldn't have to pay anything. The participants'd pay me a fiver a time, something like that.'

'Hmm . . .' Ted still wasn't persuaded. 'And it'd be your kind of music?'

'Yeah, stuff I always play, you know my repertoire. And back in the day, when I did the gigs here, it never drove anyone out, did it?'

'That's a matter of opinion.'

'Come on, you did all right out of those nights. A lot of drinks got bought.'

'Yeah, but all the profit went on providing you with free Guinness.' There was a joshing quality in the way the two men argued. They were enjoying the negotiation. Clearly, they'd known each other for a long time.

The landlord looked at his watch. 'I got to go and check through tonight's menu with Ed.'

'Oh, do say you'll let us try having the choir here, just the once,' Heather pleaded.

Carole and Jude could see that Ted was about to say no, but suddenly he relented. Maybe he was susceptible to Heather's new-found flirtatiousness. 'When do you have in mind?'

'Monday week,' Heather replied quickly. Clearly, she and KK had it all worked out. 'Go on, let us try; see what happens.'

'All right. Just the once, though. No promises of any more, till we see how that one goes.'

'You're on.' Heather beamed. 'I can't thank you enough, Ted. You're a real sweetheart.'

'I don't know about that,' he mumbled, as he went back into the kitchen. But he was clearly pleased by what she had said.

KK Rosser needed to go off to give a guitar lesson, so Carole and Jude had serendipitously achieved something they had both wanted since Leonard Mallett's funeral – the opportunity to talk to his widow on her own.

Jude was at the bar replenishing their drinks. The Polish bar manager Zosia poured two large New Zealand Sauvignon Blancs without being asked. Heather wanted a gin and tonic. 'Make it a large one,' said Jude.

Carole didn't quite know how they were going to get round to the subject they really wanted to discuss, so at first she continued the previous conversation. 'Have you been involved in another choir like the one you're trying to set up here?' she asked.

'Not really. It was KK's idea, and I thought, well, why not give it a go? I've sung in lots of choirs over the years, though. At school and university. I was at Manchester.' It was strange; for no very good reason, Carole wouldn't have imagined that Heather Mallett had been at university. 'Then, I joined some others while I was working in London, but, since I got married, it's only been the church choir.'

'Yes.' Carole recognized that this was the perfect springboard for a question about Leonard Mallett's death and funeral, but couldn't find the right way to phrase it. Fortunately, at that moment, Jude appeared with their drinks. And, smoothly as ever, she went straight to the relevant subject by saying, 'I was sorry to hear about your husband's death.'

'Thank you,' Heather replied formally. 'It wasn't totally unexpected. He was getting very frail. It's strange, if you marry someone considerably older than yourself, from the start you kind of subliminally take on board that they're likely to die before you. That doesn't mean it's not a shock when it happens, though.'

'I'm sure it doesn't.'

'Are you married, Jude?

'No. Have been a couple of times. Not currently, though.'

'Carole?'

'Divorced,' came the crisp response.

'And how are you feeling now, Heather?' asked Jude. Carole envied her gentle directness, something that was partly instinctive and partly developed through her work as a healer. Carole knew if she had asked the same question, it would have sounded brusque and clumsy.

'I'm not in too bad a place,' Heather replied. 'I don't think it's any secret that Leonard and my marriage was . . . well, let's say not made in heaven.'

'So, you actually feel some level of relief?'

'Yes, Jude. I know that's not the kind of thing the recently bereaved should say, but . . . yes, I am looking forward to the next stage of my life, to doing different things.'

'Like starting the choir here?'

'That kind of thing, yes. And of course, I'm busy helping to organize Alice's wedding. That's my main priority at the moment. Do you know Alice? She's my stepdaughter.'

'Yes, I met her,' said Carole. Then, rather pointedly, 'At the funeral.'

'Of course. Well, I'm afraid you didn't see her at her best then.'

'No,' Carole agreed, wondering if Heather was about to comment further on the incident which had galvanized Fethering.

But all the widow said was: 'Grief affects people in different ways.'

'And in Alice's case, it made her aggressive?' asked Jude. 'I'm sorry, I wasn't actually at the funeral, but I did hear what happened.'

Heather Mallett grinned wryly. 'I think everyone in Fethering heard what happened.'

'Probably.'

Again, Jude's gentle manner easily prompted further confidences. 'Alice had a very complicated relationship with her father. She's never really recovered from her mother's death. She was at a difficult early teenage stage when it happened. I tried to fill the gap, but I know I wasn't wholly successful. And Leonard was not an easy man. It's no surprise Alice's behaviour got a bit out of hand.'

Carole couldn't suppress her instinctive response to that. '"Out of hand"? I think that's something of an understatement. The girl did actually accuse you of murdering her father.'

Heather Mallett looked awkward. 'I agree, that's how it may have sounded.'

'It wasn't just how it sounded. It was what she actually said.'

'Yes. I'm afraid it was the drink talking. She was very upset and confused, and I found out later she'd got through most of a bottle of vodka before the funeral started. Still, that's in the past. And, as I say, she's about to get married. I'm hoping that will settle her down a bit. Did you meet her fiancé, Carole?'

'Briefly.'

'Roddy may come across as a bit of a buffoon, but his heart is very definitely in the right place. They've known each other for years. I think he's very good for Alice.'

'Glad to hear it,' said Carole, without much enthusiasm.

Again, Jude's intervention was less acerbic. 'It must have been tough for you, Heather, all the Fethering gossip following on from the funeral.'

'It wasn't great. Normally, I wouldn't hear much of that stuff, but I was making a very positive effort to get out more around the village, so I couldn't escape it.'

'Bob Hinkley even said the police got involved . . .' Carole dangled the thought, fishing for more information.

And she got a bite. 'That was even before the funeral. They got in touch with me on the Tuesday, because someone had contacted them, making accusations about my having killed Leonard.'

'Was it Alice?'

'Oh, good heavens, no. I'm sure she wouldn't have done that.' It sounded as though she was entertaining the idea for the first time. 'Just some local busybody with too much time on their hands, I imagine.'

'Did Alice hear about the accusation?'

'Yes, Jude, she did. I told her . . . which was perhaps not such a good idea, considering the emotional state she was in. Probably that's what prompted her outburst in the church hall.'

'What did the police actually say to you?' asked Carole, now very upfront. 'Was it on the phone, or did they come and see you?'

'They phoned first, and then came to the house.'

'What, on the Tuesday?'

'Phoned on the Tuesday. Came to see me on the Wednesday.'

'The day before the funeral?'

'Yes. They told me that this anonymous allegation had been made, and they said it was the kind of rumour they could not ignore, an accusation of murder. It was part of their job to investigate stuff like that.'

'You can see their point,' said Jude.

'Oh yes. I have no complaints about what the police did. If I ever find out who actually started the rumour, though, I might be less forgiving to them.'

'Understandably.' Jude grinned, putting Heather even more at her ease, as she probed more deeply. 'It's very nosy of me to ask this, but I've heard so many conjectures around the village, it'd be nice to know what the police actually did say to you.'

'I've no objections to answering that. In fact, I'd be glad if you would tell as many people in Fethering as possible, to put an end to all the uninformed speculation and innuendos.'

'Sure. We'd be happy to do that. Wouldn't we, Carole?'

'Certainly.'

'Very well then.' Heather sighed before she started her narrative. 'Let me just fill in the background. Leonard actually died on Monday 17 February. I went out that morning at about ten, and he was still alive at round eleven fifteen, because the postman delivered a book, which Leonard signed for. It was a valuable antiquarian book about military history – Leonard was very into that. I got back to our house – we're in the Shorelands Estate – round quarter to one. And, needless to say, in a place like that, which is a haven for neighbourhood snoopers, someone saw me put the car in the garage. I suppose, on this one occasion, I should be grateful for the surveillance, because my neighbour could time my return at exactly twelve forty-seven. Anyway, I went into the house, and found Leonard dead at the foot of the stairs. I immediately phoned for an ambulance – my call was logged in at twelve forty-nine.

'It was the view of the police, I am glad to say, that, even if I had been possessed by murderous intent, I did not logistically have time to kill my husband in that two-minute window. I was therefore fully exonerated. They apologized very politely for any stress they may have caused me. End of story.'

'But, presumably,' said Carole, who had a beady eye for detail, 'they also checked where you had been that morning.'

‘Yes, of course. My alibi. Which, I am delighted to report, matched exactly with the account I had given them. I had spent that morning in Worthing, with KK Rosser.’

‘Oh?’ Carole could not keep the surprise out of her voice. The idea of Heather Mallett having anything to do with the guitarist before they’d got together over the Crown & Anchor Choir idea seemed very unlikely. On the other hand, when told of Leonard Mallett’s death, KK had said, ‘So Heather finally did it.’

‘He was giving me singing lessons,’ the widow explained.

‘Really?’

‘Yes. As I said, I’d always been in choirs, and I hope in time to get into a set-up which is a bit more professional than the church one. The Brighton Festival Chorus is the real thing, very high standards, but you do have to audition to get in. So, I was having lessons with KK, with a view to giving it a go.’

‘How did you meet him?’ asked Carole. ‘At the Crown & Anchor?’

‘Good Lord, no. I never went to the Crown & Anchor while Leonard was alive. He didn’t approve of women in pubs. That was among many things that he disapproved of. No, I got in touch with KK through a small ad in the *Fethering Observer*. He was offering singing lessons, he was nearby, it seemed to fit.’

‘And did Leonard know,’ asked Jude, ‘that you were having these lessons?’

Heather coloured. ‘No. Each time I went to Worthing to see KK, I told Leonard I was going shopping – and had to make sure that I came back loaded with stuff from the Rustington Sainsbury's.'

Jude grinned reassuringly. 'Thank you for telling us. We will do our best to ensure that we scotch any further Fethering rumours about the circumstances of your husband's death.'

'Thank you very much.'

'Just a minute,' said Carole.

'What?'

'Can I just get the timing of what happened right?'

Heather looked less than pleased with this development. She had generously volunteered information about her brush with the police. She didn't want any nit-picking over the details. 'All right,' she said reluctantly.

'You said the police rang you on the Tuesday before the funeral and came to see you on the Wednesday . . .?'

'Yes.'

'And it was on the Wednesday that you told them about your alibi?'

'Yes.'

'So why didn't their investigations stop then?'

'What do you mean?'

'Well, the vicar . . . you know, Bob Hinkley . . . came to see us on the Friday morning, the day after the funeral.' And Carole explained that it was only then, while he was in High Tor, that he had received the message to say the police investigation was over.

Heather looked instantly relieved. 'That's easily explained. There were some other people they had to take statements from.'

'Oh?'

'KK, obviously. They needed to check my alibi with him. And he was in Holland, playing with a friend's band. He'd left the same day as I'd had my singing lesson, so he didn't know about Leonard's death until he got back.'

Carole and Jude didn't mention that they were the ones who had given him the news.

'So, I don't think the police talked to him until the Friday, the morning after the funeral.'

Carole nodded. That would fit in with the call that Bob Hinkley had received while he was at High Tor. 'One other thing, though . . .'

'What?' There was now a definite testiness in Heather's voice. She had been happy to volunteer information, but not to submit to an interrogation.

'Did the police talk to Alice?'

'Why should they have done?'

'She was the one who made the public accusation against you, wasn't she? In the church hall.'

'Yes, but, as I said, she was just in a bad emotional state.'

'But surely, after what she said – she was virtually implying that she had witnessed you killing her father . . .'

'No, she wasn't,' said Heather crisply. 'And, as it happens, there was no way she could have witnessed anything. On 17 February, Alice was in London, looking for table decorations for her wedding.'

'On her own?'

'No, with her fiancé Roddy. And yes, the police did talk to both of them on the Friday morning, and they confirmed that. So, are you now happy that neither I nor Alice had anything to do with Leonard's death?'

'Yes,' said Carole humbly, chastened by Heather's tone of voice.

'Thank you very much for telling us all that,' said Jude. 'And if we do hear any more rumours, we will stamp them out.'

'Thanks.'

'Incidentally,' Jude went on, 'if you do get this choir thing together with KK, you know, here in the pub . . .'

'Yes?'

'I'd be quite interested in joining.'

Carole looked at her neighbour in complete amazement. Where on earth had that idea come from?

Seven

The energy generated by Heather Mallett's new Merry Widow status proved very effective. Jude responded to the notice in the village newsletter and, within a few days, received an email announcing that, a week the following Monday, the first meeting of the Crown & Anchor Choir would take place. She mentioned this to her neighbour and received a predictable response.

'So, are you really thinking of going?'

'Yes.'

'Huh.' And only Carole could say 'Huh' like that.

The atmosphere in the Function Room of the Crown & Anchor was jolly from the start. Though he'd been slow to accept the idea of a choir in the pub, Ted Crisp had softened his attitude, even to the extent of lighting the fire in the Function Room and – even more unexpected – providing free wine and nibbles for the participants. 'Only for the first meeting,' he cautioned. 'Don't think this is going to happen every time.'

Heather had smiled at this. Smiled with confidence, because it implied that the landlord envisaged continuity in her project. She was very serene that evening, again dressed in clothes with some colour in them, and pleased that her idea had come so quickly to fruition.

Her co-organizer, however, looked far from

relaxed. KK Rosser, who had changed his denim jacket for a black leather one, seemed twitchy, constantly moving around while the participants were arriving, checking his chair, his guitar and an unruly cardboard folder, from which pages of musical scores spilled.

Perhaps, Jude hazarded, he was nervous because the role of choirmaster was a less familiar one for someone who had spent most of his professional life playing in front of audiences. On the other hand, he had claimed to Ted that he'd organized a similar set-up at a pub in Brighton. So, he should be used to the routine. Maybe there was another cause of his current disquiet.

Not for the first time, Jude found herself wondering about the precise nature of the relationship between Heather and KK. What Heather had said about wanting singing lessons and finding his ad in the *Fethering Observer* was plausible enough – or would have been plausible enough for someone who hadn't been married to an apparent tyrant like Leonard Mallett. And Heather had admitted to lying to her husband about where she was going when she had her lessons with KK in Worthing, having to ensure that she returned to Shorelands Estate, 'loaded with stuff from the Rustington Sainsbury's.' That was the kind of behaviour that might be expected from a woman who was having an affair.

Of course, if Heather Mallett had been having an affair, and if her husband had found out about it . . . given the fact that it was KK who had provided her alibi for the time of the death . . .

Jude knew that her mind was moving too

quickly, making random connections where quite possibly none existed. Heather and KK's relationship did bear thinking about, though. But not at that moment, not until the first meeting of the Crown & Anchor Choir had ended.

Given the casual nature of the announcement in the village newsletter, and the short notice, there was a very healthy turnout. About twelve Fethering residents were sufficiently curious to venture out of their houses into the cold March evening. Apart from Heather, all five of the church choir members who'd been in the pub after Leonard Mallett's wake were there: Ruskin Dewitt, Bet Harrison, Shirley and Veronica Tattersall and Elizabeth Browning. Having witnessed Bob Hinkley's anxiety about numbers, Jude hoped this didn't represent a permanent shift of allegiance.

Because they came from Fethering, most of the participants knew each other at least by sight, and Ted's free wine thawed any social reticence. There was a positive buzz of anticipation around the Function Room, and it took a few moments for Heather to command their attention.

'Thank you all so much for coming.' Then she gave her name, '. . . in case any of you don't know me. What we're here for today is obviously a new initiative, and the aim of the Crown & Anchor Choir is simply to have fun. I was always in choirs through school and university, and then right up until I got married . . .' She coloured, aware that everyone in the room had speculated about her marriage and the manner of its ending.

But she recovered herself and continued, 'And I always got enormous pleasure from singing with other people. For those of you who haven't done it before, well, you have only to lift up a paper these days to find another article about the health-giving effects of choral singing. If you believe what they say, it's the antidote to loneliness and depression and most of the other evils known to man. So, hopefully, the journey we're embarking on tonight will not only prove enjoyable, but also therapeutic.

'Before we start, a couple of people I want to thank. Ted Crisp, who I'm sure you all know, has not only allowed us to use this Function Room free of charge, but has also generously provided this evening's wine and snacks.' The landlord was no longer in the room. As soon as he'd opened the wine bottles, he'd scurried back to safety behind his bar. Beneath his gruff exterior, Ted was one of those innately generous people who got horribly embarrassed by being thanked for anything.

Jude was struck by how confidently Heather Mallett was addressing the group. The retiring 'invisible woman' of Fethering had been transformed into this highly competent initiative-taker. Jude found herself even more intrigued about what had actually gone on inside the Malletts' marriage.

'The other person,' Heather went on, 'to whom I owe an enormous debt of thanks is KK Rosser.' The musician gave a wave, as if he'd just completed a guitar solo. 'It was KK's idea to get the Crown & Anchor Choir going, and he is going to bring his considerable musical expertise to us in the role of choirmaster. Incidentally, for those of you who haven't heard him, KK is always very busy locally playing with his band Rubber Truncheon.'

Not that busy, thought Jude, remembering Ted Crisp's views of the subject of KK's gigs.

'Anyway,' Heather concluded, 'I'm now going to hand over to him and . . .' She stopped in response to the guitarist's gesture of mercenary finger-rubbing. 'Oh yes, I should have said: although KK was keen to give his services for free, I insisted that he must be paid something. So, he's generously agreed that each of us should pay a fiver for every session of the choir that we attend. Which I think is very good value.'

Nobody disagreed. Though there was poverty in Fethering, over on the Downside Estate, the people who lived there weren't the sort who'd be likely to join a choir. The residents of the rest of the village were typical middle-class, constantly worrying about money, but with no real reason to.

'Good, glad you're all happy with that. Well, over to you, KK.'

The guitarist seemed more relaxed now. Maybe he had just been nervous about meeting a new group of people. As he spoke to them, his voice took on a kind of laid-back mid-Atlantic twang. 'Yeah. Thanks, Heather. Sorry about having to charge you, but we all need a bit of bread, don't we? And, incidentally, first thing I want to do is to lose that handle "choir-master". Sounds really formal and uptight, and if there's one thing these sessions ain't gonna be, it's formal and uptight.

'We're just here for the pleasure of putting a few tunes together. And, if any of you are a bit nervous about performing in public, don't worry about it.'

'Well, of course, I performed a lot in public, back in my Glyndebourne days. That was before the trouble with the nodules on my—'

Possibly pre-warned by Heather, KK didn't allow Elizabeth Browning to get into her narrative stride. He continued, 'The Crown & Anchor Choir doesn't exist to do gigs, just to get together and sing. Sure, if in a while we get a good sound going and people hear it and offer us gigs . . . cool, we might do them. But that's not the aim of the exercise. We're just here to loosen those old vocal cords and make sweet music.

'And it isn't like an exam. It's not competitive. If you're a good singer, that's cool. If you're the kind who can just about hold a tune on a good day, that's cool too. And don't worry if you can't read music. I've had a full-time career as a muso for longer than I care to remember, and I can't read a note of music. Don't forget, Paul McCartney can't read a note of music either.'

No, thought Jude wryly. But then Paul McCartney woke up one morning with the complete tune of 'Yesterday' in his head, didn't he? I don't see much evidence of your having done anything like that, KK. She reflected how enduring the myth of the rock star lifestyle was, how many young men had bought into the fantasy of instinctive genius, of having no training, no responsibilities, along with an endless supply of gigs and groupies. She remembered a joke which a former musician lover had told her. 'What do you call a drummer without a girlfriend?' To which the answer was, of course, 'Homeless.' She had a feeling that KK Rosser fitted rather closely into that timeworn profile.

'Anyway, enough chat. Let's get down to some singing. You've done some photocopies, haven't you, Heather?'

'Sure.'

'Well, pass those round.'

Heather, Jude observed, had put a lot of work into preparing for the evening. The music had been assembled in black plastic folders, one for each person there, and a good few spares.

'Now, I don't know,' said KK, 'whether this is your kinda music, but it's my kinda music, and this is the kinda music we're going to be playing. Yes, sirree. It's basically stuff I like and, by the end of the evening, you're going to like it too. And if any of you think choirs belong in church and that kind of crap, well, your ideas are going to change.' Jude felt relieved Bob Hinkley wasn't present to hear this.

KK picked up his acoustic guitar and strummed a chord. 'Now you'll see the music in your folders has got the dots all printed out for you. If you can read them, great. If not, join my club. Of course, I don't know what kind of voices you've got, and I'm not too bothered about all that soprano, tenor, bass stuff. We'll just find some harmonies we like. And the best way we'll find those is by cutting the crap and starting to sing.

So, I want you all to turn to page seven on your hymn sheets – uh-uh, my little joke. Anyone know this one?'

It was Carole King's 'You've Got a Friend'. Jude joined those who put up hands of recognition. The only people who didn't were Ruskin Dewitt, and the two sisters Shirley and Veronica Tattersall. Presumably, their lives in church choirs had never encompassed popular music.

'OK, let's just start singing. I'll give you a chord, and we'll go straight into the song on the count of three.' KK strummed his guitar. 'Ah, one, two, three . . .'

They were ragged, yes, but because most of them were familiar with the song, the overall sound was not too bad. Covertly, Jude looked around at her fellow singers. Though the Tattersall sisters were very nervous and gave little voice to the unfamiliar tune, all of the other participants looked happy. Ruskin Dewitt was, as ever, serenely flat, and serenely unaware of being flat. At the end of the song, the singers gave themselves a spontaneous round of applause.

'Not so dusty,' said KK. 'We've got a good range of voices here, so let's work out how we're going to use them to get the best harmonies . . .'

As he moved around, singing the lines he wanted the individual voices to take, Heather Mallett, whose note-perfect voice had soared above the others during the song, positively glowed. Her idea for the Crown & Anchor Choir was going to be a success.

* * *

They continued work on 'You've Got a Friend' and three other songs until about eight fifteen. Then, rather abruptly, KK looked at his watch and said, 'Well done all of you. Afraid that's all for tonight. I gotta split. Due at a rehearsal.'

Jude remembered Ted Crisp's assertion that KK never rehearsed and wondered whether that had been true or was just joshing between the two men. Heather raised a hand to stop KK's departure. 'We haven't paid you yet.'

This could have been a plea to make him stay, but the woman's tone hadn't sounded needy.

'Look, I gotta dash. Could you collect the bread, Heather, and give it to me whenever?' Whether or not that implied the two were going to meet before the next Monday, Jude couldn't be sure.

But, as KK shoved his guitar into its black zip-up case and hurried off, Heather didn't look upset by his departure.

And in the Crown & Anchor bar, she looked distinctly happy. At the end of the proceedings some of the singers had gone straight out into the chilly night, but a good few had stayed for another drink. Jude was pleased about that. Though Ted had been generous with the free wine, she thought it was important to back up KK's assertion that the choir evenings would boost his takings across the bar.

'Well, that was rather fun,' boomed Ruskin Dewitt. 'I clearly have a lot to catch up on after my misspent youth concentrating on church music.'

'Never underestimate popular song,' said Bet Harrison.

'I never will again. And if you can sing one kind of music, I'm sure you can easily adapt to another kind. The basics remain the same.' Yes, thought Jude a little uncharitably, whatever the music, you still can't sing it. You are destined to be flat for ever. There was something about Ruskin Dewitt's certitude and complacency that had always annoyed her.

'Of course, a lot of the great divas,' said Elizabeth Browning, 'broadened their repertoire very considerably into different genres of music. And I remember, at Glyndebourne, we were once asked to provide backing for an album of—'

Heather had clearly been around Elizabeth long enough to know that interruption was the only way of stemming her flow. 'Will you be up for coming again, Ruskin?' she asked.

'You betcha. My expedition into the mysterious world of popular song must continue. And please, my dear Heather, do call me "Russ".'

'All right . . . Russ.'

Jude reckoned it was worth asking the direct question. 'And will you all go on doing both choirs . . . you know, this and the church one?'

'Oh yes, I'm sure we will,' said Heather quickly.

'Of course,' said Bet Harrison.

'Can't let Bob down, can we?' said Ruskin Dewitt.

With an edge of cynicism, Jude wondered how long those good intentions would remain.

'Apart from anything else,' said Heather, 'I want to have the full complement for Alice's wedding. No absentees then. Have you all got the date inked into your diaries?'

'Certainly,' said Bet.
'Wouldn't miss it for worlds,' said Russ.
Heather turned to Jude. 'And what about you?'
'But I'm not in the church choir.'
'That's a detail. You've got a lovely singing voice. I heard you in the Function Room. And I noticed you could read music.'
'Yes, but that's different. Bob Hinkley asked me if I'd join the church choir and I had to apprise him of the small but important detail that I don't have any faith.'
'Don't worry about that,' said Heather breezily. 'If all the people who have no faith stopped going to church, the congregations would be even smaller than they are already.'
'Well . . .'
'Go on, say you'll join in. I want Alice and Roddy to have the most perfect wedding it's possible to have.'
'Oh, all right,' Jude conceded. 'I'll do it for the wedding, but that's a one-off. There's no danger I'm going to become a regular.'
'That's fine. But bless you for saying you'll do the wedding. I'm so excited about it. Alice is such a lovely girl, that I want her wedding to be the best day of her life.'
Jude blinked. Was Heather really talking about the young woman who only a few weeks before had accused her of murder?

Eight

It was a week later, the following Monday morning, that Jude had a call from the Rev. Bob Hinkley. 'I hear that you're going to be singing at Alice Mallett's wedding,' he began, almost brusquely.

'Yes. Heather asked if I would. As a favour.'

'Does this mean you might reconsider my request to join the choir on a more permanent basis?'

'No, I'm afraid it doesn't. The issue of my not having any faith is still to me a considerable objection.'

'But if you make an exception for a wedding . . .'

'I'm sorry.'

'Oh, well, it was worth asking.' He sounded really harassed, nearing the end of his tether. 'It's just . . . Bet Harrison . . . Do you know her, only recently moved to Fethering?'

'I've met her, yes.'

'Anyway, she didn't appear for yesterday's service. I rang her and she said, with childcare problems, the time commitment was getting too great, Friday evenings and the Sundays. She said it was more convenient for her just to do Monday evenings with *the choir at the pub*.' He contrived to get a lot of contempt into the last few words.

'I'm sorry about that, Bob, but hopefully you'll be able to recruit other people. There must be more undiscovered singers in Fethering. Not me, though, I'm afraid.'

'Huh,' he said. Then, almost as if he was speaking to himself, 'What are people going to think if, so early into the job, I can't even keep my church choir?'

Needless to say, Carole's attitude to the Crown & Anchor Choir did not get any less sniffy. 'Oh, your pub singers are getting together for a second week?' she said when Jude mentioned it.

'Yes. The first meeting was very successful. About a dozen people turned up.'

'About a dozen people turn up to anything new in Fethering. They soon drift away, though.'

'Well, we'll have to see, won't we?'

'Huh,' said Carole.

Jude was quite surprised to get a call from Heather to ask if she could turn up to church choir rehearsal on the Friday of the same week. She repeated what she had said to the vicar, that she had only agreed to sing at the wedding and had no intention of becoming a permanent member.

'I know that, but we will actually be rehearsing some of the wedding stuff on Friday.'

'Oh, but it's still weeks away, isn't it?'

'Yes, but the music we've chosen for the wedding is quite complicated. Well, no, not complicated, it's just that I want it to be of a really high standard, so it'll need extra rehearsal.'

Jude wasn't very keen on giving up her Friday evenings as well as the Mondays, but she reasoned that it was only for a relatively short while. Her Fridays would be free again after the wedding, and she did want to give Heather any support she could. So, she agreed to turn up that week. At seven thirty. The church choir would rehearse their normal stuff first, and then do maybe three quarters of an hour on the wedding music.

It became clear in All Saints that Friday evening just how seriously the programme was being taken. Jonny Virgo had risen to the challenge. At last he was dealing with music that was worthy of his talents, and Jude could observe what a good choirmaster he must have been for organizing school concerts and other choral music events.

He started with what he regarded as the most difficult piece on the programme, the anthem which would be sung by the choir alone during the signing of the register. This was Schubert's 'Ave Maria'. Heather produced the scores for it. As she had for the Crown & Anchor Choir, she had been busy photocopying and fitting the sheets into black plastic folders, which were distributed to the choir members.

'Now, this is a very well-known piece,' said Jonny, 'which I'm sure you will have heard often, at many other weddings. But I doubt if you've ever heard it very well sung. It's notoriously difficult for amateurs. Don't worry, though, we're going to work on it so hard that, come the wedding day, we'll have you sounding like professionals!

'All right, so let's have a go at it. Those of you

who can read music, follow the dots. Those of you who can't, don't worry. And if any of you are a bit iffy about when to come in, I will give a very firm nod of my head at the relevant moment. OK, so off we go!'

Jonny Virgo's hands descended on to the organ's keyboard and rolling chords swelled up into the empty heights of All Saints Church. As arranged, Jude had joined the rest of the choir at seven thirty. Most of the regulars were there, though two notable absentees were Bet Harrison and her son Rory. The choir didn't rehearse in their stalls but gathered round Jonny at the organ.

His words about 'sounding like professionals' seemed to have had the opposite effect to what he had intended. Rather than encouraging his singers to greater efforts, the diktat had made them nervous. Heather, who sang the soprano solo part, had done some homework, but she didn't get much support from the rest of the choir, and their first rendition of the piece was pretty dreadful.

'Hm, some way to go,' the choirmaster understated, after his charges had brought the anthem to a rather ragged conclusion.

The singers looked appropriately abashed. The Tattersall sisters, in particular, who had been very quavery during the singing, now looked to be on the verge of tears. Only Ruskin Dewitt wore his customary expression of confident serenity.

'Still, early days.' Jonny Virgo got up from his organ bench and came towards the choir in the manner of someone with something portentous to say. 'Look, the wedding that we're rehearsing for is only a few weeks away. And, Heather, you want the music to be of the highest standard possible . . .?'

'Yes, I do,' she asserted.

'Well . . .' He took a deep breath. 'If we're aiming for the highest standard possible . . . then I'm afraid there's no way you can sing the solo.'

Heather's silence, and the expression on her face, showed the power of the body blow she had just received. Jude wondered how long the fantasy had been nursed of taking that role at her stepdaughter's wedding.

Jonny instantly covered himself with apology. Confrontation did not come naturally, and he had clearly built himself up for the assessment he had just delivered. 'I'm sorry, Heather, but I have your own interests at heart. If you want the best music, you've got to get the best singers available. And, though you're a good workmanlike amateur soprano, I'm afraid that solo has to be sung with more expertise.'

He stopped, the anguished expression on his face suggesting he feared her response might be physical violence.

But Heather was far too well brought-up to do anything like that. And also, she proved to be a pragmatist. 'I see,' she said, after a pause. 'Well, you're the choirmaster. You know what your requirements are.'

'Yes.' As if empowered by the tameness of her reaction, he went on, 'In the usual Sunday-to-Sunday work of the choir, I'm happy to make the best of what's available, but if you're really after quality . . .'

'Which I am,' Heather asserted.

'. . . then I'm afraid I have to take a more hard-nosed approach. In most of the choirs I've worked with, entry has been by audition, which does provide some kind of quality control. Obviously, you can't do that in a parish church.' The way he spoke suggested that he was unleashing a flow of grievances which he had been nursing for some time. 'There you have to be glad for what you can get.'

He seemed to realize that this was potentially insulting and hastened to say, 'Not that I'm criticizing your efforts. I am very grateful to all of you for your commitment and the time you devote to the choir. Your efforts add considerably to the success of Sunday services at All Saints. But . . .' He trod delicately '. . . if one is really looking for the best . . . as we are in this situation, Heather . . . then we have either to raise the standard of the voices we use or . . .'

'Or what?' asked Heather tightly.

'Or we have to content ourselves with an easier repertoire.'

'Not do the "Ave Maria", you mean?'

'Exactly that. There are less challenging pieces which—'

'I don't want a less challenging piece for Alice's wedding,' came the firm response. 'I've been determined since she and Roddy announced their engagement that they should have the Schubert "Ave Maria" during the signing of the register.'

'If that's how you feel, you have to make a choice. You can either have it not done very well or . . .' Jonny Virgo shrugged.

'Of course,' said Elizabeth Browning, 'there was a time when I could have taken the solo, no problem. But, since the nodules . . .'

'What if we got in a professional singer for the solo?' Heather suggested suddenly.

'Well . . .' Jonny hadn't been expecting that, and clearly the idea was not without its appeal. 'Obviously, if you were to go down that route, you'd have to be prepared to pay for—'

'I'm prepared to pay.'

'But where do you start looking for a professional soprano?' asked Ruskin Dewitt, who felt he had been left out of the conversation for too long.

'Of course, back in my Glyndebourne days, I had a wealth of contacts in the—'

'That's not a problem,' Jonny interrupted. 'I've still got a lot of friends in the professional ranks. And, anyway, the soloist doesn't have to be a soprano. I've heard the part done very effectively by a tenor.'

'Ooh,' said Heather, with sudden excitement. 'Maybe we could get Blake Woodruff?'

Jonny Virgo looked thunderstruck by the suggestion. Presumably because Heather was setting her sights rather high. Even Jude, who didn't know a lot about the classical music world, had heard of Blake Woodruff. He had first come to prominence as a boy chorister, when he sang the theme tune for a very successful television series. His recording had become a chart-topping single, and the image of the beautiful, ten-year-old blond boy had been inescapable that Christmas.

Unlike many such infant phenomena, Blake

Woodruff had continued to have a career as an adult. His boyhood treble had developed into a fine classical tenor. He was one of those few singers who had crossed over from the concert and operatic repertoire into the mainstream. He produced albums reinterpreting standards from musical theatre, and even made further impressions on the pop charts. He was in constant demand and spent his life jetting to concert venues all over the world.

'You're never going to get him, are you?' Russ expressed the views of the rest of the choir.

'I wouldn't be so sure,' said Heather. 'I . . . that is to say, Alice actually knows him.'

'Does she?'

'Yes, they worked together on some big charity fundraiser. I can't remember what it was in aid of, but she was with a few fellow actors doing some readings, and apparently she and Blake got on rather well.'

'Well . . .' Jonny smiled in a way that wasn't quite condescending. 'I'm all in favour of aiming for the top, Heather, but I'm not sure that you could afford the kind of fees someone like—'

'I probably could,' she interrupted. 'Whatever his faults, Leonard did leave me very well-heeled.'

This was the first time Jude had ever heard the widow voice any criticism of her late husband. From the expressions on the faces of the rest of the choir, it was a first for them too.

'Anyway,' Heather went on, 'couldn't you call in a favour, Jonny? Use the old school tie connection?'

The choirmaster looked shocked. 'I don't know what you're talking about.'

'I'd heard – that is, Alice said Blake told her that he'd been taught by you, back when he was a chorister.'

'Then I'm afraid she got the wrong end of the stick,' said Jonny sharply. 'I've never met Blake Woodruff. Goodness, music teachers are always going on about their pupils who have made it. If I could claim someone of his stature as one of my pupils, I'd be talking about him all the time.'

Heather looked confused. 'But I thought . . . I mean, I know that . . .' She changed her mind about what she was going to say, and went on, 'Maybe Alice did get it wrong. But, because she knows him, she could ask, couldn't she?'

'As I say, Heather, I think you're aiming rather stratospherically high in terms of finding someone. I know a couple of perfectly good tenors, who would do the job for you at a price that wouldn't involve a second mortgage.'

Jude reckoned that was probably an inappropriate image. If there was one thing someone like Leonard Mallett, spending a lifetime in insurance, would have done, it was to pay off his mortgage as soon as possible.

But Heather wasn't troubled by metaphors. She said, 'Surely it wouldn't do any harm for me – for Alice to ask him . . .?'

'No!' said Jonny Virgo with surprising firmness. 'Please believe that I know more about this world than you do. If you want me to find a tenor for you to sing the "Ave Maria" solo at Alice's wedding, I will find one for you.'

'Very well,' said Heather meekly. 'If you could, Jonny . . .'

Again, he seemed empowered by having won that little argument. 'There's one other thing I need to say about the composition of the choir for the wedding.'

They were all silent, as they waited for what he needed to say.

'Russ . . . I'm afraid you can't do it.'

'What?' The bearded man looked genuinely confused.

'You can't be in the choir for the wedding.'

All he could come up with was another 'What?'

'Russ, I've tolerated listening to you for years at school assemblies and in the church choir, but I'm afraid I can't have you in the choir for the wedding.'

'Why ever not?'

'Because you sing far too loudly . . .'

'Well, I've always been stronger in the horse-power department than the steering, but I'm not—'

'What's more, you can't hold a tune. You are always flat.'

There was a silence in All Saints. The Tattersall sisters looked nervously at each other. Jude got the impression that the whole choir recognized the truth of Jonny's words. They'd known for years that Ruskin Dewitt could not sing. But nobody had ever before stated it out loud.

'That's ridiculous, Jonny!' he blustered. 'Look, I know you've always been jealous, since when we were both teaching at Ravenhall, because I had a more natural rapport with the pupils than you ever did, but this is—'

'I'm sorry, Russ,' said the choirmaster, 'but you cannot sing at Alice Mallett's wedding!'

'What bloody right do you think you have to say that?' He turned to the stepmother of the bride. 'Heather, look, we've been in this choir together for years. We've always got on, and we've been involved in some damned fine performances – weddings, funerals, carol concerts, the lot. No one's ever complained before about me not being able to hold a tune. Go on, you want me to sing at Alice's wedding, don't you?'

There was a silence before Heather Mallett articulated the words, 'No, Russ. I don't.'

The bearded man slammed his plastic folder down on to the paving of the aisle and stalked out of the church.

Nine

'So, this soloist Jonny Virgo's set up,' asked Carole, 'does he start coming to rehearsals straight away?' Although she claimed to have no interest in Alice Mallett's wedding, she could not completely curb her curiosity.

'No. He'll just come to the final rehearsal, the day before the ceremony.'

'Huh,' said Carole. 'So, till then, do you rehearse just the background stuff?'

'"Just the background stuff"? What do you mean?' asked Jude.

'Well, the oohing and aahing in the background that goes on while the soloist sings.'

Jude sighed. Carole was not as totally ignorant about music as she was pretending to be. But it was entirely in character for her to behave like that when venturing into any territory where she felt insecure. Jude was of the opinion that her neighbour could actually sing, if she hadn't devoted so much emotional effort to convincing herself that she couldn't. But she was far too sensible ever to raise the issue.

'And do you think Alice Mallett really knows Blake Woodruff?' asked Carole. Jude was quite surprised she didn't claim ignorance of the famous tenor as well as everything else that appertained to music.

'I don't see why not. Alice is an actress.'

'Not a very good actress.'

'We don't know that.'

'Well, from all accounts she doesn't get much work.'

'No.' Jude did find her neighbour very tiring when she was in this contrarian mood. 'And Heather said they met at a charity function. Sounds quite plausible to me.'

'Yes. Maybe.' A silence. They sipped their coffee.

'You said you thought Heather might have known Blake Woodruff too . . .?'

'Sort of impression I got. But you'd have thought, if she actually did, she'd have made more of it.'

'Hm . . .'

'Incidentally,' said Jude mischievously, knowing exactly the response her next suggestion would elicit, 'I know you have no wish to join the choir . . .'

'I'm glad at least you've got that message.'

'. . . but they're quite a jolly bunch.'

'I'll take your word for that.'

'And most of us tend to stay for a drink after rehearsal . . . you know, round eight thirtyish.'

'So?'

'So . . . I just thought, if you were at a loose end one Monday, you might like to come down to the pub and join us.'

Carole's pale blue eyes looked bleakly at her neighbour. 'Jude, the day I join your choir friends for a drink in the Crown & Anchor at eight thirty on a Monday evening, you will know that I have exhausted all other possible demands on my time.'

'Right,' said Jude, suppressing a smile. Her expectation of Carole's response had been exactly fulfilled.

There was a silence. Then Carole, characteristically worrying away at a subject which most people would have thought defunct, asked, 'So, Heather actually stated that she could afford Blake Woodruff's fee?'

'I don't know if she had any idea how much it might be, but yes, she did say that.'

'Hm. And she said that Leonard's death had left her pretty "well-heeled"?'

'That's exactly what she said, yes.' Jude looked straight at the pale blue eyes, shielded by their rimless glasses. 'What are you implying?'

'Just that speeding up the receipt of an inheritance is one of the commonest motives for murder.'

Jude sighed again. She thought all that conjecture had gone away. Clearly, for Carole, it hadn't. And nor, she had to confess, if she was completely honest, had it for her.

The Monday before the wedding, the Crown & Anchor Choir met as usual. Bet Harrison was now a regular, though without her son Rory, but Ruskin Dewitt hadn't attended since his summary exclusion from the wedding choir. Since he lived in Fedborough, there was little danger of other members bumping into him in the streets of Fethering, but Jude did worry about the effect his banishment might have had. She knew nothing about his personal circumstances, but somehow didn't see him as married. And the enthusiasm with which he had embraced the Crown & Anchor

Choir at the start suggested that he might have time on his hands in retirement. Presumably he no longer came to the pub on Mondays because he feared a level of awkwardness when he met Heather.

Jude felt saddened by what had happened to him but couldn't think of any way of checking on his well-being. Nor could she forget the level of irritation he always inspired in her, with his bear hugs and self-absorption.

She also thought back to the slight tension she had detected between Russ and Jonny and wondered how far that animosity went back. She knew they had both taught at the same school, Ravenhall, for a while, and Jonny's attack on his former colleague's singing might have been the venting of some long-accumulated bile.

But, though the relationship between the two men intrigued her, Jude had to confess to herself that it wasn't really her business.

And the surfaces of both choirs seemed effectively to have closed over the absence of Ruskin Dewitt.

The imminence of the wedding gave an added excitement to the Crown & Anchor Choir's meeting that Monday. Though not all of those present were in both choirs, there were enough who would be at Saturday's ceremony for a giggly sense of anticipation to run through KK's rehearsal. To make the closeness of the event more real, Alice Mallett, who was staying with her stepmother till the big day, had joined their ranks. And, whatever her skills as an actress, she certainly had a fine natural soprano voice. When congratulated on it, she said, self-effacingly, 'It's not as good as it should be. I keep meaning to get singing lessons, but never get round to it. Maybe I should set up something with KK . . . or Jonny, if he's got time.'

The song they were working on that evening was 'Time of the Season', which, Jude recalled, had been a hit for the Zombies. Though she hadn't been around when it was first released in 1967, it was a tune of which she was particularly fond. She couldn't think about it without remembering an actor lover, considerably older, who had tried to entrap her in his psychedelic past. The liaison had not lasted, but it was one she looked back on with increasing wistfulness. He, of course, was long dead, but hearing the Zombies' song never failed to revive her memory of him.

The Crown & Anchor Choir had rehearsed the number before, it was a favourite of theirs, and that evening KK was pleased with their first attempt.

'That's getting quite cool,' he congratulated them. 'Almost funky. But what it should be – and what you dudes aren't making it yet – is sexy. It's a very sexy number; think "The Summer of Love". Those breathy noises over the opening should sound like you're enjoying some really good foreplay.'

Neither Shirley nor Veronica Tattersall knew where to look, so they looked at each other. And that made them blush.

'And,' KK went on, 'make those responses sexy too.' He strummed a chord on his guitar. 'So, like, I sing: "What's your name?" And you echo it, but I want that echo to sound like you're on the way to a really major orgasm.'

Again, Shirley and Veronica Tattersall didn't know where to look. They didn't make the mistake of catching each other's eye this time. But they still blushed. Elizabeth Browning, on the other hand, nodded knowingly, as if in recollection of orgasms shared with lovers long dead (no doubt at Glyndebourne).

Jude again noticed, on the first run of the song, the beauty of Alice Mallett's voice. Obviously, because they weren't related by blood, this couldn't be a genetic inheritance from Heather, but there was something about the way the two women sang side by side which implied harmony – and not just in the musical sense. The more Jude saw of them together, the more out of character seemed Alice's outburst after her father's funeral. Heather appeared as bonded to Alice as any mother could be to a daughter she had given birth to.

'OK, dudes,' said KK, 'let's just rehearse these responses. I'll sing the lines, you do the echoes. And remember, like you're having really good sex . . .'

Shirley and Veronica Tattersall didn't know where to put themselves.

Carole was feeling lonely. It was something she rarely admitted to herself. If she experienced such weakness coming on, her normal resource was to take Gulliver out for a brisk walk on Fethering Beach. And it would never occur to anyone who saw her out there that she was lonely.

Nobody who had a dog could be lonely, could they? It was the main reason she had bought Gulliver when she'd moved permanently to Fethering.

But the trouble was, that Monday evening Gulliver wasn't with her. He was at the vet's. He'd had a very messily upset stomach for the previous few days – no doubt occasioned by some noxious seaborne delicacy he had ingested on the beach, and the vet had wanted to keep him in overnight to monitor his condition. Carole was not given to sentimentality about animals, but this threat to Gulliver's health made her realize how desolated she would be to lose him.

Her other resource when such thoughts threatened had proved unavailable that evening. She had rung through to Stephen and Gaby's house in Fulham, early enough to have a chat with her talkative and increasingly articulate granddaughter Lily, but had been greeted by the voice of an Eastern European babysitter, announcing that her son and daughter-in-law were out. Lily and her little sister Chloe had been put to bed early and were both asleep. Would she like to leave a message? Carole didn't.

She tried to concentrate on *The Times* crossword, but the clues remained intractably opaque. She zapped desultorily through a few television channels but found what was on offer even duller than usual.

And then she remembered what Jude had said about some of the choir staying on at the Crown & Anchor after rehearsal.

* * *

Both Heather and Alice went for a drink in the bar after that evening's session. KK came too. He seemed completely to have shed the nervousness he had demonstrated at the Monday choir's first meeting. As he relaxed, Jude warmed to him, finding beneath the rock 'n' roll image a generous soul with genuine interest in his fellow human beings. He was just one of those people who lacked any ability to deal with the practicalities of life.

He also seemed very relaxed around Heather. Maybe, Jude conjectured, that had been the reason for his earlier anxiety. He was afraid of being seen in public with the new widow. Jude didn't know the extent of their relationship, but there was clearly a bond between them. Good for Heather, she thought. Life with the late Leonard Mallett did not sound as if it had been a barrel of laughs. His widow deserved some time in the sun.

Waiting in the bar for the choir as they came through was Alice's fiancé, Roddy Skelton, dressed in Wodehousian tweed. He rose from his table and his half-full pint of bitter to greet everyone. 'Come on, my shout. Let me buy you all a drink.'

'You don't have to do that,' said KK. 'You don't even know me.'

'Never mind. I gather most of you are going to be singing at the wedding on Saturday, so this is an early thank-you.'

'I won't be there,' KK pointed out.

'Don't even think about it. I'm just feeling extremely jolly, and I would like to share my good humour. Now, I know Alice and Heather will be on the Pinot Grigio. What about the rest of you songbirds?'

While Roddy went to the bar with his shipping order of drinks, Jude looked across the room to see a very awkward-looking Carole enter. Knowing the situation with Gulliver, and realizing how much pride her neighbour must have swallowed to come to the Crown & Anchor, she went across to give her a hug.

'Come on, quick. Roddy's buying drinks.' Jude called across to the bar. 'Could you add another large New Zealand Sauvignon Blanc!'

'Wilco!'

'But I can't accept a drink from someone I don't know,' whispered Carole, appalled.

'It's Roddy Skelton. I thought you said you met him at the funeral.'

'Well, yes, I did, but only for a moment, and that's hardly a close enough relationship for him to—'

'Too late. He's already given the order,' said Jude. 'Now, come and meet the choir.'

Mutely, reluctantly, Carole let herself be led across the room. 'I know you're worried about Gulliver,' Jude whispered. 'He'll be fine.'

Carole manufactured an appropriately subdued expression. But she had to admit to herself that it wasn't just anxiety about the dog that had brought her to the Crown & Anchor that evening. She couldn't get out of her head the scene she had witnessed after Leonard Mallett's funeral, and a visit to the pub offered her the perfect opportunity to monitor the interplay between widow and stepdaughter. Carole still wanted explanations.

The atmosphere in the alcove they'd all managed to cram into was, as Jude had promised, very jolly. The excitement generated by the closeness of the wedding still continued, and Heather reported to those who didn't know that Jonny Virgo had actually been pleased by the music rehearsal the previous Friday. 'And he's a very hard taskmaster.'

'Oh, goodness,' said Elizabeth Browning, 'don't talk to me about hard taskmasters. When I was at Glyndebourne, we had this internationally renowned conductor who—'

Like the rest of them, Bet Harrison had clearly learned the skill of interrupting whenever the word 'Glyndebourne' was mentioned. She said wistfully 'I almost wish I'd stayed with the church lot to sing at the wedding. But time, you know, is always a problem. Looking after Roddy as a single mum . . . well, it's not easy.'

Jude was beginning to wonder whether Bet ever conducted a conversation without immediately bringing up the difficulties of her marital status. Still, with characteristic generosity, she told herself that the woman's divorce was relatively recent.

'I'm sure it's our loss you won't be singing,' said Roddy with easy diplomacy. He was sitting beside his fiancée, and the two of them looked very together. Alice gazed at him adoringly. The tweed suit he wore managed to look almost as formal as the pin-stripe he'd had on at the funeral.

'Very jolly,' he went on, 'being back here in the Crown & Anchor. Scene of my first illicit underage pint.' Roddy chuckled and looked across the table to KK. 'Are you part of the singing brigade too?'

The guitarist put down the pint of Guinness from which he had been drinking and wiped the moustache of froth off his top lip.

'Well, I am, like, in the business of singing, dude, but I'm afraid I won't be at your wedding gig.'

'No worries.'

'KK's in charge of the choir we have here in the pub,' Heather explained.

'Oh, right. Gotcha.'

'I'm, like, a professional muso,' said KK.

'Right.'

'Got a band called Rubber Truncheon.' Once again, he spoke the name in anticipation of some reaction.

'Sorry, afraid I'm rather in the ranks of the tin ears when it comes to music. Heard of the Beatles and the Rolling Stones, but that's about it.' Roddy took his fiancée's hand. 'Still, Alice is musical enough for the both of us. Let's hope her talents, rather than mine, are passed on to the sprogs . . .' For a moment he looked uncertain, before adding, '. . . if we have any.'

'So, what do you do?' asked KK. 'You're not in the theatre, too, are you?' he added, in a tone of total disbelief.

'Good God, no. I'd never remember the lines. No, I'm in the army.'

'Oh.' KK's lip curled. Jude could see him about

to voice what people who regard themselves as 'creatives' think of the armed forces, but he thought better of it. All he said was, 'Well, there you go then.'

'So how did you and Alice meet?' asked Jude, easing the conversation back on to an uncontroversial plane.

'Oh, right here in Fethering. That's why I know the Crown & Anchor. We met at the Yacht Club. My Aged Ps live in Smalting . . . well, it's just my father now. My mother passed on a couple of years back, but the old man's astonishingly fit for his age. Still on the golf course a couple of times a week.' He spoke with unapologetic pride. 'So, I've always been round this area. And always loved "messing about in boats". Alice and I've known each other since we were . . . what? Fifteen?'

'Thirteen,' Alice corrected him.

'Thirteen,' he echoed. 'The lady is always right. Anyway, we got back in touch after I'd finished at Sandhurst . . . and here we are.' He chuckled heartily. 'If I'm going to get away from her now, I'll have to do it before Saturday, won't I?'

Alice smiled indulgently. There was clearly no way she was ever going to let him get away from her.

'So, Roddy . . .' Carole felt it was about time she contributed something to the conversation. 'What branch of the army do you work in?'

'Intelligence.'

Jude was glad she didn't catch her friend's eye. There was a serious danger she might have giggled. But clearly there was more to Roddy

Skelton than one might have expected on first impressions.

'And does your work take you all over the world?'

'Seen a fair bit of it, yes. Done tours in the Gulf, a couple in Afghanistan. And then of course sometimes have to go abroad for training.'

'So, aren't you fully trained yet?' KK couldn't resist asking. 'Didn't they teach you anything at Sandhurst?'

Roddy smiled good-humouredly. Whatever he may have thought inwardly, he wasn't about to rise to such rudeness. 'Oh, you never know it all,' he said, 'particularly in the world of Intelligence. Apart from anything else, the technology is changing on a daily basis. You wouldn't believe the stuff the techies are coming up with. I was on a week's course at GCHQ recently, and some of the software the Russians are developing . . .' He made a mock shudder. 'Very scary.'

'When was this?' asked Carole.

'Month or so back. Well, I can tell you exactly when it was, because I didn't finish the course. Had to come back down here a day before the end, when I heard about Leonard's death.'

'I don't suppose you can give us more detail about this Russian software . . .?' asked Bet Harrison.

'You're spot on there. I can't. More than my job's worth. Probably more than my life's worth, the way the Russians are behaving these days.' He guffawed heartily, though the danger he mentioned was quite possibly real.

'I find it really frightening,' said Bet Harrison. 'We seem to be going back to the Cold War. And I don't want my son Rory to grow up in that kind of atmosphere, you know, of international tension, fear of a nuclear holocaust. Particularly because I'm a single mum and he doesn't have a strong male role model at home.' She was back on her familiar tracks.

Jude once again diverted the conversation. 'Heather, do you know much about the tenor Jonny's booked for the wedding?'

'Not a lot. Except that he's called Toby. Jonny's worked with him before, and says he's very reliable, a safe pair of hands. And he has sung the "Ave Maria" a good few times, so he knows it well. But we'll find out more at rehearsal on Friday, won't we?'

'Jude,' Carole hissed, as they left the Crown & Anchor. 'Did you notice?'

'Notice what?'

A bunch of rowdy youths staggered out of the pub after them.

'I'll tell you when we're alone,' Carole murmured conspiratorially.

'Fine. Oh, damn,' said Jude, holding out her empty hands. 'I left my handbag where we were rehearsing! Wait. I won't be a moment.'

Carole let out a sharp sigh of irritation.

As Jude approached the Function Room door, she heard a raised voice from inside. Raised in panic and fury. 'KK,' it said, 'keep your hands to yourself! Don't you ever dare touch me again!'

Jude just had time to slip into the Ladies, leaving the door ajar, so that she was not seen by Heather Mallett as she came storming out of the Function Room.

Ten

Jude's desire to tell her co-investigator what she had just witnessed was pre-empted. Carole still stood at the edge of the pub car park, stamping her feet against the cold with ill-disguised impatience. As soon as her neighbour was in earshot, she repeated her earlier question with the same urgency. 'Jude, did you notice?'

'Notice what?'

'What Roddy Skelton said.'

'Sorry?'

'In the pub just now. About GCHQ.'

Again, Jude could only look puzzled. The headlights of a BMW, leaving the car park far too fast, illuminated the two women briefly. As a streetlight caught the driver's face, Jude realized it was the deeply affronted Heather Mallett, on her way back to the Shorelands Estate.

'Roddy,' Carole explained patiently, 'said he'd gone on a week's course at GCHQ . . .'

'Yes.'

'. . . but then he'd had to come back down here before the course ended, because he heard about the death of his father-in-law-to-be.'

'Yes,' Jude agreed again, beginning to wonder whether her neighbour was going to move on from just repeating the conversation they had both heard.

Carole did. 'Alice Mallett's alibi for the time

of her father's death was that she was in London, choosing table decorations for the wedding . . .'

'Mm.'

'With Roddy.'

Light dawned. 'Ah. I see what you mean.'

'Except, of course . . .' Carole filled in the details. 'Roddy wasn't in London. He was at GCHQ in Cheltenham. Which means . . .' She paused portentously 'that Alice Mallett has no alibi for the time of her father's death.'

Carole accepted the offer of a 'nightcap' at Woodside Cottage. It was partly that she wanted to talk further about what she was again thinking of as 'the case', but also that she wanted to put off as long as possible the moment when she had to return to an empty, Gulliver-less, High Tor.

She murmured something about just needing a cup of tea but did not protest too much when Jude produced a bottle of Sauvignon Blanc from the fridge. The fire had nearly died down while Jude had been at her choir rehearsal, but she quickly resuscitated it with kindling and vigorous use of the poker. The glow of flames flickering across the ceiling soon augmented the subdued lighting of the sitting room.

When they'd both got full glasses, Jude told her neighbour what she had heard from outside the Crown & Anchor's Function Room.

'What do you think it means? That Heather was ending their affair?'

'Hang on a minute, Carole. We don't know that there was any affair.'

'Oh, there must have been. Heather claiming

she was having singing lessons with KK – I've never heard a more blatant cover-up. There must have been something going on between them.'

'We don't know that for sure. Anyway, what I heard doesn't definitely mean she was ending an affair.'

'So what else could it mean?' asked Carole sceptically.

'It could mean that tonight was the first time KK had come on to Heather, and she didn't want their relationship to move in that direction. She wanted them just to stay friends.'

'Huh.'

'Carole, we don't have enough information to reach any conclusion about it.'

'Oh, really, Jude! And I thought I was meant to be the wet blanket in this partnership.'

'In this case, I am happy to take over the role.' Jude had her own reasons for keeping a curb on their speculations.

'If you insist.' Carole sighed in frustration. 'What we do have enough information about, though, is Alice Mallett's alibi – or rather lack of alibi – for the time of her father's death.'

'Yes,' Jude conceded.

'We must investigate that further.'

'How?'

'Talk to Roddy. Talk to Heather. Talk to Alice herself, for God's sake! Do what investigators normally do.'

'But that would be virtually making an accusation of murder.'

'If a murder's been committed, it's quite

common for the perpetrator to be accused of the crime,' said Carole sniffily.

Jude still dragged her heels. 'We don't know that a murder has been committed.'

'Oh, come on, Jude.'

'Anyway, what right have we to investigate? It's normally the police who do that sort of thing.'

'Maybe. But the police have been particularly useless in this case, haven't they?'

'How do you mean?'

'They never showed much interest, did they? They seem to have been convinced from the start that there was nothing suspicious about Leonard Mallett's death. If they hadn't thought that, they would have put some time into detailed checking of the alibis they were given. And they would have found out how easily broken Alice's was. They just didn't bother.'

Jude couldn't deny the probable truth of this.

'If a crime's been committed, and the police just sit on their hands,' Carole stated categorically, 'then it's our duty, as citizens, to investigate it.'

Carole could sometimes get very Home Office about issues like this, demanding that the right thing should be done. Jude, on the other hand, had always had a much more fluid interpretation of what was meant by the word 'justice'.

Carole did not sleep well that night. She berated herself for excessive drinking late in the evening, but knew that was not the real reason for her agitation.

So, she was hugely relieved when, sharp at eight thirty the following morning, she received a call to say that Gulliver was absolutely fine and could be picked up from the vet's as soon as she wished.

Driving there in her trim Renault, Carole thought about the state she had been in overnight. She had been genuinely worried that she would never see Gulliver again. However hard a carapace she tried to construct around herself, her feelings were still vulnerable to the many unforeseeable accidents of life. And now she had the two granddaughters, the list of her hostages to fortune had increased.

It was nine o'clock when the telephone rang in Woodside Cottage.

'Hello, Jude. This is Heather Mallett.'

'Oh, hi. Good to see you yesterday. All the wedding planning in place?'

'Yes. But that's not what I wanted to talk about.'

'Oh?'

'I wanted to talk about something Roddy said last night.'

'Ah.'

'I wonder . . . would you be free to come round here for a coffee?'

'Yes, sure. When?'

'As soon as possible.'

'Fine.' Jude was still in her dressing gown and fleecy slippers, enjoying a cup of instant in the kitchen. 'Just got to put some clothes on, twenty-minute walk . . . be with you in half an hour.'

'I could come and pick you up.' There was an urgency in Heather's voice.

'No, the walk'll do me good.'

'You know where we are?' The common widow's mistake of using the first person plural.

'I've got the name of the house, and I know the Shorelands Estate.'

'See you shortly then.'

'Fine.'

Jude had been to other houses on the estate, but never before to the Malletts'. As she passed the open main gates of the compound, she felt the customary shudder at the sight of the regulations board . . . all about how dogs must be kept on leads and washing be hung out only on certain days of the week. Not for the first time, she wondered who the noticeboard was actually there for. The residents must all know the rules by now. Which meant that the regulations were on display simply to impress on visitors the level of exclusivity of the estate they were about to enter.

Heather's house was called 'Sorrento'. Its style was 1950s Georgian, and it was on the more expensive side of the estate, boasting a garden at whose end a gate gave access to the dunes of Fethering Beach.

Heather ushered her in from the cold, through a rather old-fashioned, wood-panelled hall. Vases of fresh flowers brought a bit of colour but failed to lift the ambient gloom. Jude tried not to look too overtly at the staircase, but presumed she actually was at a Scene of Crime. It was there that Leonard Mallett must have breathed his last.

Her hostess led the way into a sitting room,

whose chintzy armchairs and sofas also dated from a previous era. Heather seemed to acknowledge this, waving a hand airily and saying, 'Once I get the wedding out of the way, I'm going to give the house a complete makeover.'

In the bay window that looked out towards the sea stood a baby grand piano. Heather seemed ineluctably drawn towards it. She brushed her hand over the keys, then picked out the opening notes of Mendelssohn's "Wedding March". 'My new baby,' she said. 'I always grew up with a piano in the house. When I was a student at Manchester, they were always readily accessible. But after I got married . . .' She didn't need to finish the sentence. 'I've just taken delivery of this. Already, I love it.' She moved reluctantly away from the keyboard.

On a low table was a tray, bearing a cafetière, two National Trust mugs and a matching milk jug. Sugar was not even on offer. So few people took it these days.

Gesturing Jude to an armchair, Heather pushed down the plunger and asked, 'How do you like it?'

'Just with milk, please.'

When they were both equipped with coffee, Heather also sat down and began, very directly, 'The fact that you agreed to come here suggests that you did hear Roddy say something odd last night.'

Jude gave a cautious grin. 'Not necessarily. It could just be the prevailing vice of Fethering, curiosity to see the inside of another resident's house . . .?'

Heather swept aside such triviality. 'Just to make sure I'm not barking up the wrong tree, what was it you heard that you thought was odd?' She was covering herself, not giving away any information till she knew how much her guest knew.

'I didn't actually pick it up immediately,' Jude confessed. 'My neighbour Carole drew my attention to it.'

'Ah. Yes. That doesn't really surprise me. Got sharp eyes, that one.' Then she said, urgently, 'So what did Carole draw your attention to?'

'The fact that Roddy was on a course at GCHQ in Cheltenham at the time of your husband's death.'

Heather Mallett nodded, accepting the extinction of a hope. But she moved briskly on. 'So, Carole – and indeed you – are aware of the implications of that?'

'Yes. It means Roddy was lying about being in London choosing table decorations with Alice on the day your husband died.'

'Mm.'

'And the alibi for your stepdaughter which he gave to the police doesn't hold up.'

'How do you know what alibi he gave?' asked Heather sharply. 'Do the police confide in you?'

'No such luck. Surely you remember? It was you who told us about Alice's alibi.'

'Yes, yes, of course,' said Heather wearily. 'I'm afraid I've talked to so many people in the last few weeks about Leonard's death, that I forget who I said what to.' She looked directly at Jude, her brown eyes probing. 'So, what – if anything – are you planning to do?'

'Do?' asked Jude, tactically obtuse.

'Yes. You now know that Roddy was lying about being with Alice on the day Leonard died. What are you going to do about it?'

'I think Carole and I would probably give different answers to that question.'

'Oh?'

'Carole used to work at the Home Office. Her attitude to public duty is non-negotiable.'

'Whereas yours . . .'

'I think I'm able to see more sides to an argument than she is.' This was said with no self-congratulation. It was simply a statement of fact.

'I'm glad to hear it. Right, in this particular argument, what sides do you see?'

'I see, I think, Heather, a lot of unhappiness in your family.'

'I'm not going to argue with that.'

'And, given the way that you have . . . come out of your shell . . . since your husband's death, I might leap to the obvious conclusion that he was the cause of at least part of that unhappiness.'

'I'm still not arguing.'

'So, you wouldn't argue if I were to say that yours was an unhappy marriage?'

Heather shook her head, tense, uncertain how to respond till she heard what came next.

'The question that raises for me is: if your husband made you unhappy, did he make his daughter unhappy too?'

There was a silence. Then Heather said slowly, 'You're a very perceptive woman, Jude. It must be down to all that healing you do.'

'It's hard to do the job without accumulating some knowledge of human psychology.'

'I'm sure that's true.' Heather sighed. 'No, I wasn't happy with Leonard. I have to say that was partly my fault. I was very wide-eyed and naïve when we met, and I was attracted by the idea of a well-established, wealthy man taking an interest in me. Leonard was never going to be the life and soul of any party, but he seemed honest and reliable. People were deferential to him at social occasions; he seemed to command a lot of respect. Basically, he offered me stability, after a series of unsatisfactory relationships with younger, irresponsible men.'

Jude said nothing, happy to let Heather control the narrative in her own way.

'So, I thought, by marrying Leonard, I would be shoring up my own security for the rest of my life. It was only after we were married that I realized how controlling his personality was.'

Jude still kept silent, thinking how many of her clients had described their marriages in almost identical words.

'He was a bully and, having done me the hugest of favours by marrying me, he then proceeded to abuse and humiliate me.'

'When you use the word "abuse" . . .' Jude began tentatively.

'I use it in the fullest sense of the word. Domestic violence, sexual assaults. As the years went by, Leonard's potency declined. He would never have considered blaming himself for that, so he blamed me. As a result . . .' For the first time in the conversation, Heather's face expressed the revulsion for what she was describing '. . . he demanded ever more extreme actions from me to stimulate his failing libido.'

'And what about his first wife?'

'What do you mean by that?' asked Heather sharply.

'I meant, do you know if there was any history of abuse while he was married to her?'

'I don't know. Leonard was the only person of our acquaintance who would know the answer to that. And he wouldn't have been about to tell me, would he?'

'No. Probably not. Just that, in my experience of clients who've suffered sexual abuse from their partners . . .' Jude had dealt with a distressingly large number of such cases over the years '. . . it rarely comes from nowhere. There's usually some history.'

'I've no idea what happened with his first wife. And I wasn't about to ask. It would only have made Leonard angrier. And who would his anger have been taken out on? No, I wasn't going to deliberately antagonize him.'

'I understand.'

'Alice, though, was fascinated by her mother, and how she'd died.'

'How old was she when it happened?

'Round twelve, I think. Leonard would never talk to her about it. She kept asking, but . . .'

'Was your husband in sole charge of her after her mother's death?'

'Technically, I suppose, yes. But she was packed off to boarding school very soon after, I think. Didn't see much of her father from then on . . . which suited Alice very well, because she loathed him.'

The two women looked at each other for a long, slow moment. Then Heather said, 'Look, all I want at the moment is for Alice to have the most perfect wedding possible. And I believe there are things you think, Jude, things you know, actions you might take . . . which could threaten that outcome.'

'What do you mean?'

'Oh, don't be *faux naïve*! You know what I mean. You were about to ask me whether Alice too was abused by Leonard.'

'I wouldn't say—'

'Yes, you would. I don't know you well, but I know your type, Jude. Once you have a suspicion about something, you worry away at it, like a dog with a piece of rag, and you won't let it go until you've got some kind of explanation.'

'That would probably be a more accurate description of Carole than me.'

'It fits both of you. The only difference is a matter of degree. But I'm not criticizing you for it. Seeking out injustice, righting wrongs, they're admirable ambitions . . . so long as they don't concern my family.'

Jude thought she now understood the direction in which Heather's thoughts were moving, but she waited until they were spelt out for her.

'I get the impression that if I told your friend Carole what I'm about to tell you, she'd go straight to the police with the information.'

'I don't know what you're going to tell me,

but that is an accurate assessment of Carole's character.'

'OK.' Heather looked down at the cafetière. 'I could make some fresh coffee if you—'

'Don't worry. I'm fine.' Tell me what you have to tell me, Jude urged inwardly.

'Right.' Heather sighed and looked down over the garden fence to the English Channel. 'Very well. Yes, Leonard did abuse Alice. And she was at a much more vulnerable age than I was when it started. It had a devastating effect on her. I talked of myself having dreadful relationships with men, but that's nothing on the scale of what Alice went through.'

'But now she's through all that, and about to get married.'

'Yes,' said Heather positively. And then, with less certainty, 'Yes . . .'

'Did Alice tell you about what had been happening?'

'No. I found out. It wasn't an easy time, for either of us. It took years for me to actually talk to her about the subject.' She looked ashamed. 'Once again, I was too afraid of Leonard to . . .'

'But when you did talk to her about it . . .?'

'At first she denied everything. But gradually, very slowly . . . I think it took her a long time to realize that we had both suffered in the same way. And that I might be on her side. Once she did start talking, though, there was no stopping her.'

'And that must have formed a bond between you.'

'You could say that, Jude, yes.'
Another silence. 'Going back to Leonard's death . . .' Jude prompted.
'Yes,' said Heather wearily. 'We have to, don't we?'
'I'm afraid so. You, I gather, have an alibi for the relevant time. Or maybe you don't? Are you about to tell me that?'
'No. I was with KK. No lies there.'
'Having a singing lesson?'
'Yes.'
Remembering what she had heard the night before, Jude curbed the instinct to ask about the nature of her relationship with the guitarist. At that moment there was a more urgent topic. 'But you left Alice in the house with Leonard?'
'Yes.'
'And do you think she killed him?'
'Yes,' said Heather.

Eleven

Jude nodded thoughtfully. 'I think I get it now.'

'Get what?'

'What happened after your husband's funeral.'

'Ah.'

'You were worried about suspicion focusing on Alice. So, you ensured that suspicion was focused on you instead.' Heather was silent. She looked very tired. 'You chose a rather histrionic way of doing it, but I can see why you did. Alice is an actress, after all. It wasn't difficult for her to act out the accusations against you.'

Heather smiled wryly. 'Well done. I can see why you're good at your job. You understand how people work.'

'Thank you.'

'And if ever I was in need of healing services – or if Alice was – we might well . . .' She stopped, apparently regretting having embarked on the sentence.

'You'd be more than welcome. I don't actually specialize in your kind of problem, but I'd—'

'Who said I've got a problem?' Heather snapped.

'You've said it. This morning. What you've told me. Unless you don't regard being the victim of sexual abuse as a problem . . .'

'Hm.' Heather nodded, taking that on board. 'At the moment I'm so confused. There's a lot of stuff in my head that I've got to sort out. But I'm not going to even think about it until I've got Alice safely married.'

'Afterwards, though . . .?'

'We'll see.'

'There are people who can help you. You don't want to – and you don't have to – live the rest of your life in the shadow of what you went through during your marriage.'

'As I said, we'll see.'

Silence again. Heather looked out, as if for comfort, towards the sea. The water was steel-grey and unresponsive.

'You took a big risk,' said Jude.

'In what way?'

'Setting up Alice to accuse you in the church hall. Why did you do it?'

'So that no one would suspect that she'd killed her father.'

'Had anyone voiced suspicions that she was responsible?'

'No. But KK told me he heard people in the Crown & Anchor suggesting that *I* might have had something to do with it. In other words, there were suspicions that Leonard didn't die of natural causes. I was worried that, if the rumours led to a police investigation, it might get too close to Alice.'

'So, you publicly turned the suspicions against yourself . . .'

'Yes.'

'. . . in the secure knowledge that KK could provide you with an alibi for the time of Leonard's death?'

'Exactly.'

'And you knew that Alice didn't have an alibi, so you got Roddy to provide a false one for her?' Heather nodded. 'That was another big risk you took.'

'Why?'

'Well, if the police investigation had been a bit more thorough . . .'

'I was banking on the fact that it wouldn't be.' There was now a note of pride in the woman's voice. 'I needed to stop the rumours going round Fethering. As you know, in a village like this, rumours can grow and fester and get bundled up with other rumours. So, I reckoned, if there was a police investigation which found that there was nothing to investigate, that would be a pretty good way of stopping them once and for all.'

'So, you were the anonymous caller who told the police there was something to investigate?'

'Well done. You're spot on.'

Jude shook her head. 'Still an enormous risk.'

'Maybe.' Heather spoke now in a tone of self-congratulation. 'But it worked, didn't it? The police investigated, and they concluded there was nothing to investigate. And when did you last hear a rumour round Fethering that Leonard's death was anything but natural?'

Jude didn't think it was the moment to point out that rumours in Fethering were never killed off that easily. Instead, she conceded that, yes, the dangerous strategy had paid off. But it still seemed to her a very elaborate way of going about things. And then she reflected that Heather Mallett was probably very naïve. Her sequestered life at Sorrento during her marriage had cut her off. Only someone out of touch with the real world could have dreamt up the denunciation scenario at the wake. And, Jude reckoned, Alice, the unsuccessful actress, the drama queen, would have been happy to play along, particularly with a scheme that should exonerate her from any suspicion.

'And now,' Heather went on, 'the only people who are threatening to disturb that happy situation are you and your neighbour Carole.'

'Hm.'

'You say I took a risk by setting up Alice to accuse me after the funeral. But, of course, I've taken a bigger risk this morning.'

'By telling me all this?'

'Yes. In fact, I'm taking the same risk as I did with the police. I'm volunteering information, in the hope that, by doing so, I will stop an investigation in its tracks.'

'You think, now I know the circumstances, I, like the police, will take no further action?'

'That's what I'm hoping for.' The woman looked tense; hardly surprising given how much the response mattered to her. 'Or have I read your character all wrong, Jude?'

'No. You haven't read my character wrong. From what you've told me about your husband – which, incidentally, I have no problem with believing – I cannot feel any regret for his death. Nor, indeed, can I feel very inclined to blame your daughter for helping him on his way.'

'Are you saying that you'll keep quiet about what I've told you this morning?'

'I certainly don't feel a sense of duty to tell anyone. I have strict rules of confidentiality with my clients, you know. I'm quite good at keeping secrets. And you're right. I don't have a black and white view of justice.'

'Unlike your neighbour.'

'True.'

'So, what I'm asking you, Jude – begging you – is that you don't tell any of this to Carole.'

'Till after the wedding?'

'No. Ever. You must never tell any of it to Carole!'

Jude nodded slowly. She sympathized with the woman, but she also knew how terrier-like her neighbour could be when she suspected information was being kept from her. 'All right,' she said. 'I'll do my best.'

'I'm going to ensure that Alice has the best wedding day any girl has ever had,' said Heather Mallett. 'And if anyone tries to prevent that from happening, I'll kill them!'

Though she would never have used the word – or indeed confided in anyone how bereft she had been feeling – Carole was ecstatic to have Gulliver back. Again, the strength of emotion surprised and slightly worried her.

On the Wednesday, she'd taken him for his customary early morning walk on Fethering Beach, and he got the bonus of a second outing because she needed to do some shopping on the parade. Walking back, Carole had to pass Starbucks, and she did so with her usual sniff of disapproval at the fact that it was no longer Polly's Cake Shop.

Through the window, she was surprised to see someone she recognized. Sitting alone at a table, with a large black coffee in front of him, was Roddy Skelton. Carole decided to suspend her instinctive revulsion for the place and enter. She had heard from fellow beach walkers that dogs were allowed inside.

This was her first visit to any Starbucks branch. Carole Seddon had a perverse prejudice against the popular. She didn't like to be seen doing what other people did. For this reason, she avoided chain restaurants. For her to be seen in a McDonald's or a Kentucky Fried Chicken, she would regard as social death. She felt the same about watching *Coronation Street*, *EastEnders* or *Strictly Come Dancing*. In the face of such trends, she liked to maintain her individuality. The fact that no one would ever notice if she went to a fast-food outlet, and no one would ever know what was watched on the High Tor television did not change her deep-held convictions.

But, of course, that Wednesday morning, Carole had a higher purpose. So, she entered Starbucks with Gulliver and, quickly working out that you ordered at the counter, asked for a black coffee. She saw no sign of Bet Harrison; maybe the woman worked a different shift. Offered the choice of espresso, Americano or filter, she chose filter. Carole Seddon knew where she was with filter coffee. And, ignoring the Starbucks special names for the available sizes, she said she'd have a small one.

While she waited for it at the other end of the counter, she looked around at the clientele. Huh, whatever happened to loyalty, she asked herself, as she recognized many of the regulars from the Polly's Cake Shop days. Though she knew who quite a few of them were, there were only a couple to whom she felt she had to give the minimal local greeting, a 'Fethering nod'.

Roddy Skelton did not appear to have noticed her arrival. He sat, vague and disconsolate, looking out of the window. Carole felt no guilt in walking straight up to his table, coffee in one hand, Gulliver's lead in the other and saying, with uncharacteristic heartiness, 'Penny for them?'

Roddy looked up. He recognized but couldn't place her.

'Carole Seddon. We met on Monday night in the Crown & Anchor.'

'Oh, yes,' he said, still uncertain.

'Mind if I join you?' asked Carole, in a manner that was even more out of character. She sat herself opposite before he had time to object.

Anyway, he was far too well bred to make a fuss. 'Nice dog,' he said. 'Aged Ps always had Labradors. Not now. They were getting a bit frail, so they didn't get a replacement after the last one popped his clogs. And now, of course, my mother's gone too. I think the old man misses having a dog about the place. What's this beauty called?'

'Gulliver.'

'Ah. Nice name.'

'Alice not with you today?' asked Carole, realizing as she said it that it was rather a stupid question.

But Roddy appeared not to notice. 'No. Things to do. Wedding-related, needless to say. She and her mum have got it all worked out, nothing left for me to do. Alice said she wanted me around down here in the run-up to the big event, so I took the leave, but . . . they seem to have the whole shooting match sorted out, down to the last detail. I feel like a spare prick at a wedding.' He seemed suddenly to realize the appropriateness of his words. 'Oh, rather good, eh?' And then, a little crestfallen. 'That is, pardon my French.'

'No worries,' said Carole, to her own great surprise. She had never said 'No worries' before in her life. She went on, 'I imagine it's been a rather stressful time for you, the last few months.'

'What, you mean, with the engagement, wedding arrangements, all that?'

'I was thinking more of Leonard Mallett's death.'

'Ah, yes, of course. So close to the wedding, I agree. Very sad.'

She tried fishing for information. 'And always particularly sad, isn't it, when you don't know the actual cause of someone's death . . .?'

'We do know. He fell downstairs.'

'Yes, but do we actually know what caused him to fall downstairs?'

For the first time in their conversation, Roddy gave Carole a rather old-fashioned look. Maybe, she worried, her approach had been a little too direct, in the circumstances.

'I do wish people would stop talking about it,' he said, with sudden bitterness. 'Alice is upset enough, as it is. I suppose we should have realized that, in a place like Fethering, there's bound to be a lot of gossip, but it's getting her down. People don't seem to talk about anything else.'

'I'm sorry to hear that,' said Carole, who had no more intention of changing the subject than she had of flying. 'But you have to admit that the way your fiancée behaved after the funeral was . . . well, likely to cause comment.'

'I agree. Don't know what came over her. But Alice was in a bad state, you have to make allowances. She was obviously grieving for her father. Then she'd had too much to drink. And what she actually said wasn't that bad.'

'I was there, Roddy. I heard exactly what she said.'

'Ah.'

'You and I did meet then, at the wake, very briefly.'

'I'm sorry. I . . . Rude of me to forget. There was a lot going on.'

Carole was not going to be guilty of saying 'No worries' again. Instead, she told Roddy it wasn't important. 'What was important, though, was what happened on Monday night.'

'*This* Monday night?'

'Yes. When we were having drinks in the Crown & Anchor.'

'I don't recall anything important happening then,' he said uneasily.

'The business about you having been on a course at GCHQ at the time Leonard Mallett died.'

'Ah.' He looked even more uncomfortable.

Carole felt pretty sure that his future mother-in-law had pointed out the indiscretion to him.

She elaborated. 'Which of course means that you weren't with Alice, choosing table decorations in London at the time. Were you?'

He shook his head. 'No.'

'So why did you tell that lie?'

'I don't know.'

'Oh, come on.'

'All right, I know why I told the lie. Because Heather asked me to. But why she wanted me to do it, that I don't know.'

Carole looked at him, a typical product of the English squirearchy and minor public school. Dressed in tweeds and a shirt with large checks. And yet Roddy Skelton worked for Intelligence in the Army. Could he really be as boneheaded as he appeared?

'Doesn't it seem an odd thing for her to ask you to do?'

'I don't know,' he said again. 'Look, I've known Alice's family a long time. Since I was in my teens. But, at the same time, I hardly know them at all. I certainly never knew what went on inside her father's head. And I'm kind of aware that both Alice and her mother have had difficulties . . . you know, psychological problems. All I do know for sure is that I love Alice and, once we're married, I'm going to make every effort I can to keep her from ever going back to the dark places where she has been.'

This was quite a speech to come from the mouth of someone like Roddy Skelton. Carole felt it was one of those many occasions when

Jude would have come up with a better response than she could. All she said was: 'That's very admirable.' And then, because there were some things she just couldn't leave alone, she went on, 'You must know Alice pretty well.'

'I certainly hope so. I'm marrying her on Saturday.'

But Roddy's attempt at levity didn't deflect his interrogator. 'So, you must have a pretty accurate idea of what her relationship was with her father.'

'It's not something we've discussed. We're much more interested in *our* relationship. That's what matters to us.'

'I'm sure that's the case. But, still, given the uncertainty about how Alice's father died, there must—'

'There is no uncertainty about how Alice's father died. He fell downstairs. Accidentally.' Roddy was talking with new authority. For the first time, Carole could see him giving orders to the troops under his command. Behind his blimpish façade, there was a deeply serious person.

Still, she wasn't about to be put off by this discovery. She demanded, 'How do you actually *know* that his death was accidental?'

But she'd gone too far. Roddy Skelton rose to his feet and, with considerable dignity, announced, 'I'm afraid this conversation is at an end.' And he walked out of the Starbucks.

'I thought we'd agreed you weren't going to tell Carole anything.' Heather's voice, from the other end of the line, was distinctly angry.

'I haven't told her anything,' Jude insisted.

'No? Then why do you suggest she collared Roddy this morning and virtually accused Alice of murdering Leonard?'

'I had no idea that she had done anything of the sort.'

'Well, she did. In Starbucks. So, God knows how many other Fethering gossips were listening in.'

The 'other Fethering gossips' hurt. It was identifying Jude as one of their number. 'Heather, please believe me, I have said nothing to Carole since you and I spoke yesterday. I haven't even seen her. I had clients booked in yesterday afternoon and this morning.'

'Hm.' Heather clearly still didn't believe her.

Jude had hardly put the phone down from talking to Heather, when Carole rang.

'Look, I spoke to Roddy Skelton in Starbucks this morning.'

'I know.'

'How do you know?'

'Just had a call from his mother-in-law-to-be. Virtually accusing you of harassing him.'

'I wasn't harassing him. I was just trying to get at the truth about Leonard Mallett's murder.'

'We don't know it was murder . . .'

'Yes, we do. And what's more, I'm pretty sure I know who the murderer is.'

'Who?' asked Jude wearily.

'Alice Mallett,' said Carole. As Jude had known she would. 'And I don't think that's going to be difficult to prove.'

'Oh? And how are you going to set about proving it?'

'I'm sure Heather knows more than she's letting on.'

'Look, Heather is up to her ears with preparations for her daughter's wedding and—'

'Her *step*daughter's wedding. And I think it's that relationship which is at the bottom of this mystery.'

'There *is* no mystery,' said Jude plaintively and, she knew, hopelessly.

'No? Come on, Jude, where's your instinct for justice?'

Jude couldn't think of an answer that wouldn't sound flippant, so she said nothing.

'You're not keeping anything from me, are you?' With Carole, paranoia was never far below the surface.

'No, of course I'm not.' Jude shouldn't have been surprised at being put on the spot so soon.

'Are you sure Heather hasn't said something to you, something that might clarify the position, might help us to prove how her husband died?'

Though Jude at times had the same flexible approach to mendacity as she did to justice, she found it very hard to lie in this situation. The temptation to tell her friend and collaborator the truth was almost overpowering. But she gritted her teeth and said, 'No.'

'Well, I think you're being extremely unhelpful, Jude,' said Carole.

The words hurt. Torn by conflicting loyalties to the two women, Jude felt uncharacteristically miserable. Though in some circumstances she had told white lies to avoid causing suffering, she did not take naturally to duplicity.

Twelve

The wedding morning dawned beautifully. It was one of those May days which held promise that there really would be a summer soon.

And the florists that Heather Mallett brought in had somehow contrived to make the forbidding vastness of All Saints Fethering look more welcoming. The bride's beautifully cut dress made her curvaceous rather than dumpy, and the groom looked better and generally more trim in his dress uniform than he did in civvies. It turned out that he was a Major, which Shirley Tattersall, who for some reason knew about these things, said meant he was no slouch. Making Major before thirty was apparently quite a feat. So, Roddy Skelton couldn't be as stupid as he appeared to be.

At the back of the church, a group of equally smart uniformed friends from his regiment were ready to form a guard of honour, so that the couple could march out under raised swords at the end of the ceremony.

And, proud in the front row on the groom's side, was a tall old man with black eyebrows, who could only be the object of Roddy Skelton's hero worship, his 'Aged P'.

Bob Hinkley conducted the service with appropriate gravitas and what sounded like genuine affection for the participants.

The church choir excelled themselves. As at the funeral, Heather Mallett had chosen to take her place in the choir stalls, rather than the body of the church. And she joined in a lusty rendition of the two hymns that she and Alice had spent so long choosing. They had finally plumped for 'Praise My Soul the King of Heaven' and 'Jerusalem'. Safe, maybe, but tunes they both loved. From her position at the altar, Alice's clear soprano could also be heard distinctly.

And the choir had ably supported Toby the tenor as they sang Schubert's 'Ave Maria' during the signing of the register.

Jonny Virgo had demonstrated his talents at the organ as he played the music for the entry of the bride and the newly married couple's exit from the church. The first piece was an arrangement of Jeremiah Clarke's 'Trumpet Voluntary', and the final one the very traditional Mendelssohn's 'Wedding March'. Though she didn't know much about classical music, Jude could appreciate Jonny's virtuosity. She wondered whether there had been a point when, before resigning himself to being a teacher, he had contemplated a career as a professional musician. And whether making that compromise had added to the neuroses of his later life.

He had arrived in good time before the ceremony, leading his frail mother and an elderly friend who was going to look after her during the service. He explained to the choir that Heather, who was at that moment checking arrangements outside the church, had readily agreed to his mother attending the service, 'because the old dear does so like listening to me play.'

Mrs Virgo was almost skeletally thin. Parchment-like skin stretched tightly over the sharp bones of her face, and cocktail-stick legs looked inadequate even to bear her light weight. She had arrived at the church in a wheelchair, pushed by the friend, but once she was out of it, her mobility, with the aid of a stick, did not seem to be too badly impaired.

And she was very smartly turned out. Under the camel-hair coat she wore against the cold could be seen a dress of pink silk, and her thin feet were encased in smart court shoes. Her sparse white hair had been skilfully shaped by a hairdresser's lacquer. And she clutched a large brown handbag, as though it were a lifebelt in stormy seas.

But when Jonny introduced her to the choir, it was clear that her mental capacity did not match her physical fitness. She looked vague and uncomfortable, not taking in the names her son relayed to her. She kept peering anxiously at him, worried that he was about to abandon her, and when he had to take up his position at the organ, she was very distressed as her friend led her to their pew.

From the choir stalls, Jude had a very good view of the old lady, whose agitation seemed to grow as the church started to fill up. She kept half-rising from her seat, only to be gently pulled back by her friend. But the minute her son's hands touched the keyboard to play the first notes of pre-ceremony music, Mrs Virgo settled back into peaceful, listening mode. And when Jonny started playing the 'Trumpet Voluntary', the old woman looked positively beatific. She remained in that state of calm throughout the service.

Toby, the tenor whom Jonny had brought in to handle the solos, proved to be very amiable. His professionalism had the effect of raising the choir's talents in the direction of his own, and Jude could see Heather glowing from the quality of the sounds they were producing. Any residual regret that she wasn't leading the 'Ave Maria' as soloist seemed to have long gone.

In fact, Heather Mallett glowed with satisfaction at the realization of all her dreams for Alice's perfect day. Her meticulous planning had paid off.

Though she had not invited the choir to the reception, Heather had demonstrated her loyalty by offering them a glass of champagne in the church hall straight after the ceremony. The same invitation had been offered to Bob Hinkley, and when all of the other guests were milling outside the church waiting for the bride and groom to be photographed, Heather whispered to her fellow singers, 'Come on, quick! I'll get you sorted out with a drink before I'm needed in the pics.'

The choir appreciated this priority treatment and were soon all equipped with champagne glasses. They looked around in amazement at the transformation of the church hall. The florists who had done such wonders in the church itself, had also worked their magic here. The tables laid for the wedding breakfast sparkled with gold and silver. Jude couldn't help wondering who had actually bought the decorations. She knew they hadn't been purchased by the bride on the day of her father's death. And once again she felt a pang about the difficulty of keeping secrets from the terrier-like Carole.

'Listen,' said Heather. 'I can't stay, but I did just want to say thank you enormously for all your hard work. You really brought up the standards of the church choir, and showed what we could do when we really set our minds to it.'

'I hope,' said Bob Hinkley, 'that now you've proved how good you can be, you'll aim for the same quality every Sunday at All Saints.'

'That might be tough,' said Heather. 'We put in a lot of extra rehearsal. And, of course,' she gestured towards Toby the tenor, 'we did have professional help.'

'Something I could have provided,' Elizabeth Browning reminded them, 'in my Glyndebourne days. Before the nodules.'

'But,' Bob went on, 'we should aim for those standards all the time. We do want everyone to do their best in the service of Our Lord.'

As the vicar remonstrated, he reached out a hand to touch Heather's arm. She recoiled as if she'd received an electric shock and turned on him, 'I'm not sure that everyone, Bob,' she almost spat the words out, 'thinks that the church choir is as important as you do!'

Jude was amazed by this sudden outburst, and Bob Hinkley looked shocked too. Heather tried to make up for lost ground too. 'I'm sorry. I didn't mean—'

Further apology was prevented by the arrival of Jonny Virgo and his mother, whose wheelchair meant they had made slower progress from the church than the others. Her friend, whose services as a pusher were no longer required, had presumably gone home. The old lady looked completely relaxed now she was once again with her son, and Jude was reminded of her level of dependence. The pressure on Jonny, as her sole carer, must have been enormous.

Heather grinned, her recent retort to the vicar forgotten, as she welcomed the new arrivals. 'But here's the man we really have to thank,' she said, all charm. 'Mrs Virgo, you must be so proud of your son.'

The old lady smiled a benign but unfocused smile.

'And, Jonny, thanks so much for recommending Toby. He's a star! You can keep your Blake Woodruffs, can't you?'

Jonny Virgo smiled awkwardly.

'Well done, Toby,' Heather went on. 'Alice was very impressed, I could see she was. She's the one who knows all about Blake Woodruff, of course. I introduced them. I used to know him very well at one stage in my life and . . .'

She seemed to pull back on what she was saying, and continued, 'That is to say, he's really Alice's friend. She actually invited him to the wedding, but unfortunately, he couldn't come. Touring Australia, which, as excuses go, is a pretty good one. Blake and Alice are very close.

He confides everything in her. All his guilty secrets, all about everyone who's ever been in love with him. I think he's always found it easier to attract love than to give it.' Heather chuckled. 'But if he'd been in All Saints today, he would have witnessed the work of a serious rival. Toby, you're at least as talented as Blake Woodruff!'

'Thank you,' said the tenor wryly. 'I don't know about his talent, but I wouldn't mind having a share of his royalties.'

All of the choir members giggled, except for Jonny Virgo, who looked distant and abstracted. Heather's attention was drawn by someone waving to her from the doorway. 'Sorry, I'm needed for the photos. Permanent records of this wonderful day. And thanks again to all of you, whose singing was such an important contribution to the day's wonderfulness.'

Once the main body of wedding guests came into the church hall, the choir dispersed. Jude didn't contact Carole to tell her how the event had gone, and Carole resolutely pretended that she wasn't interested, so the phone in Woodside Cottage did not ring for the rest of the day.

On the next day, the Sunday, though, it did ring, soon after nine o'clock. A bleary Jude answered.

'Did you hear what happened?' Carole was high with incredulous excitement.

'What are you talking about?'

'A body's been found, washed up on Fethering Beach.'

'When?'

'Earlier this morning. I took Gulliver out for his walk, and there was an area of the beach screened off by the police.'

'Could you see what had happened?'

'No.' There was a wistfulness in Carole's voice, as she said, 'They wouldn't let me close enough.' She soon regained momentum. 'But I met another dog walker and she'd met the person who actually found the body.'

'Oh yes?' said Jude, with a level of scepticism. She could hear the wheels of Fethering gossip clicking into motion.

'No, really! And she recognized the body.'

'Who was it?'

'Heather Mallett.'

Thirteen

'Another Fethering Floater,' said one of the sages who always propped up the Crown & Anchor bar on a Sunday lunchtime. His name was Barney Poulton; he was invariably dressed in a thick-knitted fuzzy jumper, and was assumed by non-locals – particularly American visitors – to have been a fixture in the pub from the time when it was built. He represented the salt of the earth, the old village values of a Fethering long gone. (Though he had, in fact, retired to the area only four years before, from Walton-on-Thames in Surrey, whence he had commuted for nearly forty years to a solicitors' practice in Holborn. His habit of installing himself, as a guru of local affairs, in the same bar seat most days of the week caused the Crown & Anchor's landlord considerable irritation.)

'You reckon?' asked that same landlord, wearily, from the depths of his scruffy beard.

'Bound to be, Ted,' the sage nodded, secure that no one could question his authority on local matters.

A 'Fethering Floater' was the name given to a body found on the beach there. But not just any body. A corpse washed in from the English Channel would not qualify. The 'Floaters' were ones who'd fallen into the Fether. The river was still tidal as it entered the sea at Fethering and the flow could be ferociously strong. By some bizarre combination of currents and tides, the body of someone who had fallen into the Fether would always turn up within twenty-four hours on Fethering Beach. And that, the Crown & Anchor sage assured his audience at the bar, was what had happened to Heather Mallett.

'How can you be certain?' asked Jude, who had come to the pub in the hope of getting more details of what had happened (though she was fully aware that the accuracy of such details could be extremely suspect). Carole wasn't with her, because she had been asked if the police could visit her to tell them anything she might have seen on Fethering Beach that morning. She claimed the intrusion was a great nuisance, but had been clearly excited by the prospect of giving her testimony.

'You take my word for it,' said Barney Poulton. 'I know about these things.'

Which hardly counted as concrete evidence.

'It's strange,' said Ted, 'to think she was only in here on Monday, with the choir. And I never got much impression of what she was like.'

'I don't think anyone did, really,' said Jude. 'She was quite a complex woman.'

She was surprised how shaken she had been by the news of Heather's death. Given what she knew about Alice's guilt, she felt there had to be some connection. She looked out towards the sea. The weather was as good as it had been the previous day. A few hardy souls were even sitting at the tables in the pub's garden, bordering on the dunes of Fethering Beach.

There was nothing to be seen there of the recent police activity. Heather's body had been washed up at low tide. The police screens had been set up around it, but the returning sea had forced them to move their operations – and the body – elsewhere.

'Of course,' observed Barney Poulton, sharing more of his wisdom, 'her husband didn't die that long ago.'

'No. Back in February,' Jude confirmed.

'So . . . delayed shock, do you reckon?'

'How do you mean?'

'Well, you know, like, grief. Her husband's dead, her stepdaughter's married. She suddenly realizes she's on her own, so she tops herself by jumping into the Fether.'

'That's not the way I see it,' said Jude. 'She was positively glowing at the wedding ceremony yesterday.'

'And no mother/stepdaughter conflict like there had been at the funeral?'

'Absolutely not, Barney. Rather the reverse. The two of them couldn't have been closer. And if you go back to Heather's husband's death . . . well, she seemed to be relieved rather than upset by it.'

'You can say that again.' Jude didn't know the woman who chipped in, but her clothes and vowels suggested she might be another resident of the Shorelands Estate. 'I was at the wedding yesterday and, let me tell you, Heather was in sparkling form. No, if she fell in the Fether, she certainly didn't do so deliberately.'

'I was only there at the beginning of the reception. Did she drink a lot?' asked Jude.

‘Not more than would be appropriate for the mother of the bride,’ said the woman, rather reprovingly.

‘Sorry, we haven’t met. My name’s Jude.’

‘Ramona Plowright. My husband’s Commodore of the Yacht Club.’ Clearly not one of those women who objected to being defined by her spouse. She went on, confirming Jude’s earlier conjecture, ‘We live up on the Shorelands Estate. Virtually neighbours of the Malletts.’

‘And do you know,’ asked Jude, hoping she didn’t sound too much like an investigator, ‘what Heather did after the wedding?’

‘No, Len and I left before she did. We offered her a lift, but she said she’d got stuff to do and would sort out a cab.’

‘What time would this be?’

‘Oh, I don’t know. Tennish. Weddings go on so long these days. Church ceremony, reception, and then the young ones want to dance into the small hours. Fortunately, the church hall regulations mean that the music has to stop at half past ten, and they’re pretty strict about that, but even so . . . Len and I had no wish to be party poopers, but he’s got a bad back, so we didn’t stay to the bitter end.’

‘And were the newly-weds going straight off on honeymoon?’

‘No, spending the night at the Craigmullen.’ A recently opened five-star boutique hotel, converted from a former girls’ school on the edge of the Downs between Fethering and Fedborough. ‘Roddy apparently stayed there the Friday night, and his best man drove him into Fethering for the wedding. So, his car would be at the hotel, and the plan was that they'd drive off to Heathrow this morning. Then fly to . . . I don't know, Maldives, I think it was. Though, given the circumstances, I can't imagine they've gone.'

'No,' Jude agreed.

'Absolute tragedy, isn't it?' said Ramona, feeling that perhaps she hadn't expressed adequate sympathy. 'So awful for Alice, to lose both parents so close together. Well, Heather wasn't her birth mother . . .'

'I knew that,' said Jude.

'. . . so, for the poor kid it must be like being orphaned twice.'

Any response to this was prevented by the arrival of Carole, flushed both by excitement and the pace at which she had scuttled from High Tor to the pub.

While Ted Crisp, unasked, poured another large New Zealand Sauvignon Blanc, Jude introduced her neighbour to Ramona Plowright. Barney Poulton, Carole already knew – and she found him just as much of an irritating poseur as Ted did.

'We were just talking about Heather,' said Jude.

'And we reckon her death,' Barney pronounced, 'was definitely suicide.'

'Speak for yourself,' said a rather riled Ted Crisp.

'No, you take my word for it,' the bar-room sage insisted. 'She threw herself into the Fether.'

'We don't know that for sure,' said Jude.

'In fact, we don't know very much,' Ramona contributed.

'No, but maybe Carole does know something.' Jude gestured towards her friend, as if inviting her to take centre stage. 'She's just been interviewed by the police.'

Even Barney Poulton looked impressed by that. Carole gave Jude a rather old-fashioned look, to indicate that she'd been intending to discuss the matter *à deux*, but the excitement of having a larger audience proved too compelling.

'So, what did they say?' asked Ted.

'Well, they wanted to talk to me, because I was on the beach early this morning with Gulliver – that's my dog. And they wondered if I'd seen anything untoward.'

'And had you?' asked Barney.

'No.' She still sounded disappointed. 'I only talked to another dog walker who'd met the dog walker who'd actually found the body.'

'Incidentally,' said Jude, 'were the policemen who interviewed you the same ones who were in touch after Leonard Mallett's death?'

'No,' said Carole dismissively. 'Even if it was part of the same investigation – and they gave no suggestion that it was – it's only in crime fiction that the same Detective Inspector and Detective Sergeant work on the same cases all the time. I'd never seen either of these two before.'

'So, did they talk about suicide?' asked Barney.

'No, they didn't. But they did say they were conducting a murder investigation.'

'Murder? What made them think that?'

'The marks on Heather Mallett's neck,' said Carole. 'She was dead before she went into the Fether. She had been strangled.'

Fourteen

'I didn't want to tell all that about the police in front of everyone,' said Carole, when they got back to Woodside Cottage. They had stayed in the Crown & Anchor for one of Ed Pollack's excellent Sunday roasts. Jude had suggested going back to her place for a coffee, but when they arrived, produced an open bottle of Sauvignon Blanc. Carole made only minimum demur before accepting a glass.

'You seemed to be enjoying it,' Jude responded.

'One has to put up a front when one's with people. Anyway, I suppose I didn't tell them anything important.'

'You mean there *was* more important stuff?'

'Well . . .' Carole was forced to admit, 'No, not that much. The other dog walkers must've given the impression I'd seen more than I had. The police weren't actually with me very long.' She sounded disappointed.

'Ah.'

'They asked me how well I knew Heather Mallett. To which the answer was: hardly at all, really. They'd have done better talking to you.'

'I didn't know her that well,' Jude protested.

'No? You were in two choirs with the woman.'

'Yes, but she wasn't the kind to give much away about herself.'

'No?' This one was more pointed. Carole couldn't possibly know about the confession about Alice that Heather had made. Could she? Jude felt awkward and guilty. In the new circumstances of a murder, Carole was going to be much more curious about the dealings her neighbour had had with the dead woman. Jude's ability to keep secrets would be sorely tested.

And the testing started straight away, as Carole asked, 'Did you ever spend time with Heather, just the two of you?'

'Erm . . .'

But fortunately, Jude's decision about whether to tell a direct lie was delayed by her phone ringing. 'Hello?'

'Jude, this is Alice Mallett.'

'Oh. I was terribly sorry to hear the news.'

'Not half as sorry as I was.'

'No, but I'm sure—'

The newly-wed cut across her sentence. 'I need to talk to you,' she said.

Carole was miffed when she heard who the call was from, but she couldn't summon up an argument that would justify her staying to witness the encounter between her neighbour and the bereaved bride. 'You will tell me what she says, won't you?' she demanded, as she moved reluctantly towards the front door.

'I will tell you as much as I can.'

'And what's that supposed to mean?' came the sniffy response.

'It means that I'll you as much as I can. It's possible that Alice Mallett wants to consult me as a healer. If that's the case, of course there would be an issue of client confidentiality.'

'Oh, poppycock!' said Carole. 'You always fall back on that when you're just basically being secretive. Anyway, the girl's stepmother's just been murdered. The first thing she does is hardly going to be to consult a healer, is it?'

'I can't think of a time when she might have more need of a healer.'

'No, but . . .' Carole gave up the unequal struggle. 'Just remember, I can always tell when you're keeping information from me.'

Which didn't make Jude feel any better.

'We couldn't have met at Mum's place,' said Alice. 'I've just come from there, and it's crawling with police officers. I told them I had to nip out for some shopping. I don't know whether they believed me. They may have followed me here.'

The possibility was alarming to her, and made the poor girl look even more ghastly. The radiant bride of the day before had been reduced to a dumpy, tear-stained mess, dressed in a hoodie, jogging bottoms and trainers. Her eyes were puffy from crying, and she didn't look as if she'd slept for a month.

'But,' she went on, 'it was important that I should talk to you before the police do.'

Jude nodded slowly. 'I think I know why. Heather told you that she'd told me . . . about your father's death?'

Alice nodded, too overcome for a moment to speak. Then she said, 'And, given the awfulness of what's happened to Mum, the thought of all that being revived . . . I couldn't stand it.'

'If you're worrying about my telling the police what Heather told me, put your mind at rest. She shared that in confidence, on the understanding that I would keep it to myself. And I promise you I will do that.'

'Thank you. That's one small relief, but everything else . . .' The girl's eyes filled with tears.

'It must be terrible. I can't imagine how you're feeling. Heather was in such wonderful form yesterday.'

'Yes. Wonderful.'

'When did you last see her?'

'After the dancing finished. After we'd said goodbye to everyone. Our best man, who fortunately doesn't drink, had said he'd drive Roddy and me to our hotel.'

'And did Heather say what she was going to do?'

'She said she'd had too much to drink to drive. I suggested she called a cab, but she said it was such a lovely evening – which, of course, it was – that she'd walk back to Sorrento. Which I suppose is what she did. And, on the way, she met . . .' Alice shuddered and dissolved into tears.

Jude put her arms around the girl's heaving shoulders. 'Crying's the best thing you can do. It's better to express emotion than bottle it up.'

'I know. I still can't believe what's happened; keep thinking it must have been a dream, that soon I'll wake up and . . . But I won't. That dream will be the reality for the rest of my life.'

'At least you've got Roddy by your side to help you through it.'

'Yes.' Alice looked uncertain. 'But Roddy's not . . .'

'Not what?'

'Not as stable as he may appear to an outsider. Nobody does a tour of duty in Afghanistan and comes away totally unscathed. He's . . . well, his way of coping is to build up this hearty exterior, behave as if he doesn't take anything seriously, but . . . he's not always like that. Sometimes, he just loses it and . . .'

'Are you talking PTSD?'

'He'd never admit that, and he refuses to go and have any treatment for it. His whole attitude is based on never admitting to weakness. I think it's something to do with his relationship with his father. The old man prides himself on never showing emotion, and Roddy tries to do the same. Which means he bottles things up and, when he does let go . . .' She seemed about to say more but thought better of it.

There was a silence. Then Jude said, gently, 'Heather did tell me about your father, about how he behaved towards you . . . and her.'

'Yes, she said she'd told you.' The girl shuddered. 'This is all his fault, everything. He's the villain in all this. We'll never escape his evil shadow. He's still controlling us, from beyond the grave.'

'Are you suggesting your stepmother's death is connected with your father's?'

'It must be. The two happening so close, it's too much of a coincidence for there to be no link.'

'But there isn't the obvious link.'
'What do you mean?'
'The killings weren't done by the same person, were they?'
Alice's red eyes turned on Jude, as she took in the impact of this. 'God, no! I didn't kill her. I loved her. She saved my life. I was so alone, after I lost my birth mother. Without Mum's support, I'd never have got through.'
'But do you have any idea who might have killed her?'
Slowly – perhaps too slowly – Alice said, 'No.'
Jude let the silence settle before saying, 'Do you mind if I ask you about the circumstances of your father's death?'
'No.'
'I was just wondering . . . why then?'
'What do you mean?'
'You'd suffered abuse from him . . . what, from your childhood onwards?'
'I can't remember a time when he wasn't . . . touching me.' The girl shuddered involuntarily.
'But life must have been better once you had Heather in the house. You say she saved you. You had an ally.'
'Yes.'
'And then you moved away from him, moved to London, and you had Roddy to support you. Things must have been better.'
'Yes. The hurt was still there, the damage could never be undone, but yes, for the first time I could see that I had a possible future.'
'So, I go back to my original question. Why then? Your feelings against your father had been

building up for years. Perhaps your desire to kill him had also been around for years . . .?' Alice nodded. 'Then what drove you over the edge on the seventeenth of February?'

'Two things.' She corrected herself. 'No, one thing, really. That lunchtime I was alone in the house. Mum was having her singing lesson – well, she'd told Dad she was doing some shopping, but I knew she was with KK. And Dad had gone off to some regular pub lunch with some old insurance cronies. He did that quite often. And I . . . I suppose I was feeling more confident. I'd got Roddy, the wedding date was set. So, I did something I'd never done before. I searched Dad's study.'

'Really?'

'And there I found, amongst a whole lot of other stuff . . . my mother's death certificate.' Jude held her breath, allowing Alice to tell the story at her own pace. 'It had been completed following a coroner's inquest. It said she committed suicide.'

'So, you thought your father must have abused her in the same way that . . .?'

'What else is there to think?'

There were other possibilities, but Jude didn't raise them, as Alice went on, 'I waited for him to come back. He was drunk; he always was when he came back from meeting his insurance lot. He smelled of beer. I remember, as a child, when he . . . when he came into my bedroom . . . he always smelled of beer. I can never smell beer without thinking of . . .

'He called out to me when he came in through the front door. I'd been down for the weekend, he knew I was still there. I said I was upstairs. I don't know if he thought that was some kind of come-on. I didn't say I was in his study. I can still hear his footsteps coming up the stairs, just as I heard them when I was a child. He always used to pause on the half-landing, and I used to hope that he'd change his mind and go back downstairs . . . but he never did.

'I waited to come out of the study until he was at the top of the stairs. He looked furious. "What the hell have you been doing in there?" he shouted.

'"I've been finding out how you killed my mother," I replied. And then, I just went straight forward and pushed him. He was off-balance. He fell immediately. I heard his head banging against the banisters, again and again, as he went down. I knew he was dead. And I thought it was very fair. Primitive justice, if you like. A life for a life, though of course he'd destroyed more than one life.

'Then I went downstairs, stepping over his body, not even checking whether he was still breathing. I knew he wasn't. And I watched television until Mum came back.'

The reliving of the experience seemed to have calmed the girl. She looked almost serene, forgetting for a moment the second, more recent, death. Jude could feel nothing but sympathy for her. She felt more determined than ever that Carole would never know how Leonard Mallett died.

Alice's serenity did not last. Quickly, the pain returned to her ravaged face. She looked at her watch. 'I must go back to Sorrento. Face the music

. . . or do I mean the police?' Her look became pleading. 'And, Jude . . .'

'I'll never tell them.'

'Thank you.'

As Alice Mallett rose to leave, Jude asked, 'Is Roddy back at the house?'

'No.'

'Oh? Where is he?'

A new layer of fear spread across the girl's face. 'I don't know.'

'What do you mean?'

'The fact is, last night . . .' She chose her words carefully. 'We had a row.'

'I'm sorry. Back at the hotel?'

'At the Craigmullen, yes.'

'It must have been a very stressful day for both of you.'

'Perhaps.'

'And did this happen before, before you heard about Heather's death?'

'Yes. It was only about an hour after the dancing finished in the church hall. The best man drove us to the hotel. They'd made an effort with the room . . . champagne and . . . Then we argued and . . . Roddy walked out. Our room looked out over the car park. I saw him get into his car and drive off.'

'You've no idea where to?'

'No.'

'And you haven't had a call, a text or . . .?'

The girl shook her head. 'I didn't sleep. I felt terrible. I kept texting him, but . . . Then, before seven, the police were at the Craigmullen, with the news about Mum.'

The two women looked at each other. Neither voiced the thought, but both suspected that Roddy must somehow be involved in Heather Mallett's murder.

Fifteen

Carole could not pretend to be anything other than disgruntled. She would have hotly denied that she was at the window watching for it, but she did happen to see Alice Mallett's departure from Woodside Cottage. Of course, she was far too proud actually to ring Jude. But she was desperate to know about the conversation which had just taken place next door.

She waited the rest of the Sunday for Jude to come round to High Tor. Or at least to ring. But she waited in vain.

By the Monday morning, the murder had become public property. Even the front page of Carole's sedate *Times* featured a photograph of Heather Mallett, and the tabloid headlines went mad. 'MOTHER OF THE BRIDE MURDER!' was one of their milder efforts. But, as ever, the police gave little indication of which way their enquiries were heading.

For the next few days, Fethering locals complained – but were secretly very excited – about the amount of media attention their village attracted. There were noticeably more people out and about, walking along the Parade and Fethering Beach, on the off-chance that their opinion might be solicited by a passing camera crew.

And still Carole heard nothing from Jude. Her frustration grew. By the Wednesday she had become determined to conduct an investigation of her own.

'Rare sight,' Ted Crisp greeted her, 'you in the pub at lunchtime. On your own.'

'Yes, well, I seem to have been cooped up in the house too much the last few days.'

'New Zealand Sauvignon Blanc?'

'Just a small one.'

'I think we'd better make it a large one. And I'll just charge you for a small one.'

'Oh, Ted, you shouldn't.' But it was only a token demurral. Just before noon was early for Carole to be drinking. But she was on a mission, which she thought justified behaving out of character. She was pleased to see that her calculation of the timing had been accurate. There were very few customers – even Barney Poulton hadn't arrived yet to dispense his infuriating homespun wisdom – which gave her the perfect opportunity to pick the landlord's brains.

'I assume the Crown & Anchor Choir didn't happen on Monday?'

Ted Crisp looked surprised. 'I thought you'd know from Jude that it didn't.'

'Oh, I haven't seen her for a couple of days,' said Carole airily.

He made no comment, though he knew that the relationship between the two women went through phases of *froideur*. He also knew that such phases were almost always Carole's responsibility. During their brief affair – which was never mentioned and still seemed slightly unbelievable to both of them – Ted had got some insight into the complexities of Carole's personality.

'Hardly surprising,' he said, 'is it? Given what happened to Heather. The choir was so much her baby, I would think that'll be the end of it now. Can't somehow see KK pushing on on his own.'

'Maybe not. Oh well, the vicar will be pleased.'

'Sorry?'

'Bob Hinkley was very worried about the Crown & Anchor Choir taking singers away from his church choir.'

'I didn't know that. Don't know him that well, actually. Not a regular pub-goer. From what I've seen of him, he seems like a camper to me.'

'"Like a camper"? I don't think he's gay.'

'No, I didn't mean that, Carole.' Ted chuckled, as he always did before delivering one of his jokes. '"Camper" – "In tents". "Intense". He always struck me as being very intense.'

'What a loss you were to the stand-up circuit, Ted,' said Carole drily. 'Mind you, I agree about our vicar. He does take himself very seriously.'

'I suppose, if you're the kind of bloke who does take himself seriously, being a vicar is a natural fit, isn't it?'

'Yes, but some of them do have a lighter side. I think Bob Hinkley sets himself impossibly high standards. He's an idealist.'

'Not a good thing to be in this day and age,' said Ted sagely. 'Can only lead to disappointment.'

'Yes, it can't be easy for him. Anyway, Ted, I really wanted to ask you about KK Rosser.'

'Oh yeah?'

'He didn't turn up on Monday, expecting the choir to be here, did he?'

'No. He rang me, asking if I thought anyone'd turn up. I said no. He wasn't surprised.'

'You know him quite well, don't you, Ted?'

'Well, I've known him, on and off, for a good few years. But, of course, that's not the same thing as knowing him well.'

'Do you know if he was married?'

The landlord shrugged. 'I think he may have been some time in the past. So far as I know, he's had a fairly chequered relationship history. Part of the rock 'n' roll image he so carefully maintains. Used to pick up girls at gigs; he was always talking about groupies, though how much of it was just bullshit I never really knew. Anyway, he's probably getting a bit old to do too much of that these days. But I'm sure he still thinks of himself as a babe-magnet.'

'Hm. You don't know what his relationship with Heather was, do you?'

Ted chuckled knowingly. 'You're very transparent, Carole.'

She reacted as if this was an insult. 'What do you mean?'

'Casually coming down here late morning, like you never normally do. Casually bringing the conversation round to the subject of a woman who's just been murdered. Casually asking about her relationship with someone I know. You're off on one of your investigations again, aren't you?'

Carole coloured. 'I'm just intrigued. As everyone else in Fethering is. It happened right here on our doorstep. Go on, Ted, you can't deny it. You're intrigued too.'

'No, I can't deny it. We all want to know whodunit. But I think you want to know a bit more than the rest of us.'

Carole could not fault the accuracy of his assessment. So, she just said, 'All right, I'm not denying that either.'

'You're a bit of a Rottweiler when you get your teeth into something like this, aren't you, Carole?'

'Guilty as charged.'

'You and Jude.'

'Not always with Jude,' came the frosty response. 'I am capable of investigating things on my own.'

'Yes, I'm sure you are.'

'Go on then, Ted. What do you reckon the relationship was between Heather and KK?'

The landlord shrugged. 'Well, you know they met because she wanted him to give her singing lessons?'

Carole nodded. 'Is that something he's done often, give singing lessons?'

'I think he's had an ad in the *Fethering Observer* for some time. How much take-up he's got from it, I don't know. Basically, KK's always hard up. Being bad with money is another part of the rock god image. If he could have afforded it, KK would've been the sort to spend thousands on cocaine and driving sports cars into swimming pools. But he's never had that kind of cash. And he's never made much from his gigs. That Rubber Truncheon set-up; I think sometimes he was paying the pubs to let them perform there. And, having a pathological aversion to actually getting a proper job, KK will only allow himself to do stuff that's music-related. Giving singing lessons, I guess, to his mind kind of qualifies.'

'But it was strange the way Heather did the singing lessons.'

'Howja mean?'

'She kept them secret from her husband. When she went off to see KK, she told Leonard she was just going shopping.'

'I didn't know that. No reason why I should, mind.'

'No. But the way Heather was behaving was exactly the way a wife would if she was having an affair.'

'Oh, I see where you're heading. Actually, I've seen where you're heading for the last five minutes. You're asking me if I know whether KK Rosser and Heather Mallett were having an affair.'

'That's exactly it.'

'Well, the answer's no.'

'No, they weren't having an affair?'

'No. No, I don't *know* whether or not they were having an affair.'

'Oh.' Carole sounded really deflated.

Ted looked up as the door opened to admit a party of some dozen index-linked pensioners. 'Business calls.'

'Quickly, before you serve them. Do you have a phone number for KK?'

'Sure.' He scribbled it down on a menu pad and handed the sheet across to her. 'Watch yourself, though, Carole. He's a bit of a ladies' man.'

She blushed deeply, as the landlord chuckled and went along the bar to greet his new customers.

Carole sat at a table with her Sauvignon Blanc. She was aware of her isolation and reminded herself that she never really had been a 'pub person'. A third of the contents were still in the glass when she returned to High Tor.

But it was still enough to give her a headache. She castigated herself for drinking so early in the day.

While she was doing a healing session, Jude was very careful to keep the answering services on her landline and mobile silent. For what she was doing to work required total concentration. So, on the Wednesday afternoon, it wasn't till after she'd finished treating a retired policewoman with long-term back pain that she picked up the message from the Rev. Bob Hinkley. She rang him straight away, as requested.

'Oh, thank you so much, Jude, for getting back to me. I wanted to talk to you about what's happened in the village . . . you know, since last weekend.'

'Heather Mallett's murder, you mean?'

'Yes, I suppose I do. It's just . . . an event like that is bound to be a terrible shock, not only to those immediately involved, but to the wider community.'

'Undoubtedly.'

'And if the church can't provide support to people at a time like this, then what is the church for?'

Jude knew there were cynical answers available

to this rhetorical question, but it was not in her nature to voice them.

'I feel it's a test of me, as a vicar, to provide what succour I can.' Jude was getting the impression that Bob Hinkley regarded everything as a test of him, 'as a vicar'.

'I think people do know,' said Jude soothingly, 'that the church is there, as a source of support, a place they can turn to in time of need.'

'They do perhaps know that in theory, but their track record for turning to the church in time of need is not great. I don't feel that I am the first person they turn to. I mean, look at the size of the congregation in All Saints on a Sunday.'

'Well, we do live in an increasingly secular age,' Jude waffled reassuringly. 'Traditional habits are changing, and people perhaps have different resources in times of trouble.' She phrased the next bit carefully. 'I'm sure the people who believe the church is there for them will turn to it.'

'That's not good enough,' said the vicar sharply. 'I feel I have to be more proactive than that. I have to go out into my flock to support them.'

'I'm sure that won't do any harm,' said Jude.

'Anyway, the reason I'm contacting you . . .' She had been wondering when he would get to this point '. . . is that I believe you know Alice Mallett.'

'Well, I've met her a few times. I'd hardly say I *know* her.'

'You were the first person she came to see after she heard the news of her stepmother's death.'

Jude did not question how the vicar knew this.

She had lived in Fethering long enough to know that no one could go anywhere there without their movements being observed. It was a constant source of amazement to her that some people managed to conduct extramarital affairs in the village.

'Alice came to see me,' she said, 'to discuss something Heather had told me in confidence.'

'I don't suppose you could let me know what . . .?' he fished.

'No. I said, "in confidence", and that's what I meant.'

'But now Heather's dead, surely the situation is different and—'

'In that particular respect, the situation has not changed.'

Bob Hinkley sighed. 'It's so difficult to find out anything in this place. I did contact the police, and I told them it was important that I, as vicar, responsible for the whole parish, should be kept up to date with developments. They were very unhelpful.'

Jude clucked sympathetically. She herself, on many occasions, had had cause to regret the unwillingness of the 'proper authorities' to share their findings with amateurs.

'So, what you're saying, Jude, is that you can't give me an inside line to Alice Mallett?'

'No. I can give you her mobile number if you like – you've probably got the landline number on the Shorelands Estate – but I can't do more than that.'

'I'm sure the poor girl must be in a terrible state . . .'

'I don't doubt it.'

'. . . and it's just at such times that people need spiritual support, they need to know that people are thinking of them, that people are praying for them.'

'Maybe,' was the strongest affirmation of this view that Jude could come up with.

There was a silence, then the vicar started on another approach. 'Did you hear that Alice's fiancé, Roddy, had disappeared?'

'I did hear that, yes.'

'Suspicious, don't you think?'

'I hadn't really thought about it.' She reckoned – though a considerable underestimation of the truth – that was only a white lie.

'I feel so bad,' said Bob despondently. 'Saturday was such a happy day. So full of hope.'

'I agree. I think we're all feeling bad.'

'I'm a solutions man myself,' he confessed, 'always have been. Where I worked before, in my previous employment, if there was a problem, I didn't sit around thinking about it. I've never been a navel-gazer. I always took practical steps to improve the situation. I was proactive. Then I received the call to follow Christ and to further His work, and I tried to apply the same thinking to this job. And it just doesn't work the same way. I keep setting up initiatives and . . . the energy just keeps slipping away.'

'It's difficult,' Jude sympathized, 'to get anything new happening in a place like Fethering.'

'I'm not trying to introduce anything *new*! I'm trying to *reacquaint* people with something that's been around, that has transformed the world, for over two thousand years. But I just don't seem to be doing it right.'

'Have the difficulties you've encountered,' asked Jude gently, 'had any effect on your faith?'

'Have they weakened it, do you mean?'

'Yes, exactly that.'

'Good heavens, no! They've made it stronger. Let me tell you, if the early evangelists had let minor setbacks put them off, the Christian Church wouldn't exist. No, Fethering is a challenge that has been set for me. God is testing His servant. And His servant will, in time, prove equal to the test.'

'I'm sure you will,' said Jude soothingly.

Another silence. Then the vicar said, 'The music for the wedding on Saturday was wonderful, wasn't it?'

'It was.'

'It just shows, if everyone pulls together, if everyone makes an effort, anything can be achieved.'

Jude nodded. She approved of the principle, though she had not always seen it work out in practice.

'And I don't suppose the experience of singing with the choir on such a splendid occasion made you think that you might like to participate on a more regular basis . . .?' His words slowed down as he spoke them.

'I'm sorry, no.'

'No,' he echoed, sounding disappointed. Jude was afraid that the Rev. Bob Hinkley was doomed always to be disappointed. 'I wonder whether I'll still have a church choir six months from now.'

'Oh, I do hope so.'

'So do I. But . . .' His tone grew angry. 'Heather starting up the pub choir with that layabout guitarist was a real body blow to me. Bet Harrison, who'd only just joined us, left straight away. Which meant that her son Rory went too. And at the wedding, Heather implied she might be doing the same thing. She made me so furious when she said that! She was deliberately trying to undermine everything that I was trying to set up for the parish!'

Jude was surprised by the vehemence of his anger. Surely, the animus he felt against Heather Mallett wasn't sufficient for him to have killed her . . .? It couldn't be a case of 'the vicar dunit' . . . could it?

Jude, as a shrewd observer of human psychology, knew that stranger things had happened.

Sixteen

'Friend of Jude's.'

'Oh yeah?'

'Jude from the Crown & Anchor Choir.'

'Right.'

'We met Monday before last. In the pub. After your choir session. My name's Carole.'

'OK.' KK Rosser still didn't sound convinced he knew who was at the other end of the line.

'I was ringing about Heather Mallett's death.'

He groaned. 'You and everyone else.'

'Oh?'

'The bloody cops have been pestering me like I was a paedophile. And most of the pub choir lot have been on to me.'

'Oh, has Jude?' asked Carole, fearful that her friend might be sharing with others the secrets she was withholding from her.

'No, she's one of the few that hasn't. They're all the same, pretending to share condolences, but in fact just trying to find out if I know any more about the subject than they do. Everyone round here's so bloody nosy. One of the big drawbacks of country life. Are you calling on the same mission?'

Carole hotly denied the truth of his assessment. 'I would like to meet up and talk to you, though.'

'About Heather?'

'Well, yes, but—'

'When?' he asked cautiously.

'As soon as possible.'

He backed off. 'Bit tricky today. I'm having a new amp delivered, ordered it from Gear4music. Means I'll have to stay in the flat until it arrives.'

Whether this was true, or just a device to put her off, KK was clearly taken aback when Carole said, 'That's not a problem. I could come to your place.'

As she got into her immaculately clean Renault, she remembered Ted Crisp's warning about KK Rosser. But Carole was undaunted. She reckoned she could deal with 'ladies' men'. And, anyway, she told herself, not even the most desperate 'ladies' man' wasn't going to look at her more than once.

Carole didn't know exactly what she was expecting to be the habitat of an itinerant musician who embraced the rock 'n' roll lifestyle, but it certainly wasn't a first-floor flat in a Victorian terrace, whose exterior was painted in smart wedding-cake white. Worthing was full of surprises. Despite its image as a dowdy, bungaloid 'God's waiting room', there were little pockets of architectural splendour.

KK buzzed her in on the entryphone. When she got up to the landing, he had already opened the door for her. He was in his uniform denim, and he looked at her with a mixture of defiance, curiosity, and something else which might have been fear.

He stood back for her to enter the narrow hall and gestured towards the sitting room. She had been anticipating hippy chaos but found the level of tidiness to be almost up to High Tor standards. The flat's ownership was defined by a row of six guitars fixed neatly on the wall which faced the broad front window. There was a smell in the air of recent smoking, not quite like tobacco, sweeter and more herbal.

KK pointed her towards a sofa, and made a desultory offer of tea or coffee, which she refused. Then he draped himself over a chair with one leg crooked across the arm, looking almost too elaborately casual. 'So, what's all this about?' he asked.

'As I said on the phone, it's about Heather's death.'

'*What* about her death, and why is it any business of yours?'

Carole had thought, during the drive from Fethering, how she might answer this question, so she produced her prepared reply. 'It's just, there's a lot of malicious and uninformed talk about the murder going around Fethering, and I feel I have a community duty to put a stop to it.'

Such a statement might have been plausible coming from the mouth of the Rev. Bob Hinkley, but no one who knew Carole would have thought it genuine coming from her. Using 'community' in a positive sense was just not something Carole Seddon did. She reckoned the word was the kiss of death to any project.

KK Rosser, though, didn't know her, and took her words at face value. Not that that stopped him from sounding suspicious. 'Very admirable,' he said, before adding ironically, 'what lucky dudes we'd be if everyone else showed the same level of public-spiritedness. "Community duty", eh? Anyway, this "malicious and uninformed talk" you were on about . . . presumably it concerns me?'

'A lot of it, yes,' Carole replied. She had no basis for saying this, really. Her isolation from much of the Fethering 'community' meant she was out of the loop on a great deal of village gossip.

'You don't have to tell me the kind of things they're saying.' KK sighed wearily. 'I'm already getting great blasts of it on social media.'

Not for the first time, Carole wondered whether she was missing a trick by not indulging in Facebook or Twitter. Not to use socially, of course – the idea appalled her. But for investigative purposes, that might be justified.

'I think,' she said boldly, 'the reason they're badmouthing you now is because your name came up a lot in discussion around the time of Leonard Mallett's death.'

'Because Heather was having a singing lesson with me when it happened?'

'Exactly.'

He grimaced. 'You'd think people would have better things to do with their time, wouldn't you? Except in Fethering, of course, they don't. You can only spend so long cleaning your car and counting your pension money, can't you?'

Carole couldn't decide whether this shift of pronoun from 'they' to 'you' was deliberately aimed at her or not, but she didn't react. She just asked, 'You said on the phone that the police have interviewed you . . .?'

'Oh yes, endlessly. The pigs always have a go at anyone who leads an alternative lifestyle.' Carole looked around the defiantly middle-class sitting room but made no comment. 'And soon as I say I'm a guitarist, they immediately start accusing me of all kinds of stuff . . . peddling drugs, you name it. And this time, because I'd also been questioned when Heather's old man turned his toes up . . . well, they had a right go at me.'

'It wasn't the same policemen, was it?' Carole was unwilling to have her theory, about only fictional detectives working together all of the time, blown out of the water.

KK reassured her instantly by saying, 'No. Never seen any of this lot before. Mind you, pigs are hard to tell apart, even at the best of times. And this wasn't the best of times, let me tell you.'

'So, did the police say anything to you about the two cases being connected?'

'They're never going to do that, are they? Always going to give you the absolute minimum of information. But the fact that they talked to me again . . . well, there's no other reason for them doing that, is there?'

'What do you mean?'

'Look, I had nothing to do with Alice's wedding, did I? I wasn't in Fethering the day Heather died, was I?'

'Where were you?'

'I was doing a gig with Rubber Truncheon over in a pub in Kent, wasn't I?'

Carole thought about his words. Kent and

Sussex weren't that far apart. Presumably a music gig in a pub wouldn't go on much beyond closing time. Heather was seen alive by the last guests at the wedding, so was presumably killed some time in the early hours. KK's alibi didn't completely rule him out as her potential murderer. But all she said was, 'I'm sure you know that there's been much speculation in Fethering about your relationship with Heather.'

'Tell me about it,' he groaned. 'Bloody nosy curtain-twitchers, every last one of them.'

'Well, given that she was known to be in an unhappy marriage . . .'

'Yes, yes, all right. But look, it is possible for a man to spend time with a woman without immediately groping her. All I was doing was giving her singing lessons. Coming on to someone you're teaching is a sure way of losing the gig. Heather wasn't my type, anyway. Too quiet, self-effacing for my taste. And deeply neurotic. I always go for the rock chicks. Girls who just wanna have fun. They're what lights this particular daddy's fire. They're what gets my mojo working.'

Carole had great difficulty in not wincing openly when he said this. But she pressed on. 'The fact remains that someone in Fethering witnessed you coming on to her.'

'Never!' He sounded genuinely shocked by the idea. But then that was exactly how he would have sounded if he was lying. 'When was this?'

'Monday before last.' Carole was sure of her facts. 'After the choir rehearsal. After we'd had drinks in the bar. You went back with Heather to the Function Room. And then she shouted at you to "keep your hands to yourself".'

'Oh, Jesus,' he said, sinking his balding head into his hands. The ponytail dangled hopelessly over his collar.

'Are you saying Heather didn't say that?'

'No, no, she said it. And let me tell you, it was the first time I'd ever touched her. Never once in all the times we'd met for the singing lessons had I even shaken her hand. Then that evening, I wanted to wish her luck for the wedding, and so I tried to give her a hug, just friendly, you know. But the minute I touched her, she bawled me out, just like your local snitch reported. I've no idea why. Heather was one confused woman.'

Carole digested this information, then again changed tack. 'Did the police check your alibi in the pub in Kent, in full detail?'

'Yes, of course they bloody did!' Suddenly he shouted off into the flat's interior. 'Miff! Miff, come here a minute!'

There was a sound of coughing, which grew closer. The door to the rest of the flat opened to reveal the spidery figure of a middle-aged man in grey hoodie, jogging bottoms and bare feet. He looked as if he'd just been woken up. Carole remembered that when Jude had first introduced her to KK, they'd discussed a mutual friend called Miff. She wondered if this scruffy individual was another of Jude's lovers. Carole wouldn't put it past her.

'Yeah, whassup, KK?' the man asked blearily.

'This lady's called Carole. This is Miff, drummer with Rubber Truncheon, also guy I was working in Holland with a few months back. Miff is currently without a girlfriend, which means he's been crashing out on my floor for, like, four, five months now, is it?'

'Yeah, right. I am looking for somewhere, KK.'

'Never mind that now, Miff. Will you tell this kind but nosy lady what you told the police when they asked you the same questions? Where were you every time Heather came here for singing lessons?'

'Well, I was here, wasn't I? I never get up till the afternoon. I'm a drummer, aren't I?'

'And where were you on Saturday night, after we got back from the gig in Kent?'

'I was here too, with you, wasn't I? Downing a few bevvies, smoking a bit of weed . . . well, I didn't tell the pigs that last bit, did I?'

KK grinned at Carole without humour. 'There. Are you bloody satisfied? About my alibis? For both bloody murders?'

'Yes, yes, of course,' Carole replied primly.

But her suspicion of KK hadn't completely evaporated. She still thought it odd that he had so readily agreed to meet her. As if he wanted to sound her out, to find out how much she knew.

And his assurance that he'd only touched Heather once . . . she certainly wasn't going to believe that.

Seventeen

'I believe it,' said Jude.

'Why? KK's got a reputation as a "ladies' man". I don't believe that waste-of-space drummer was around every time he gave Heather a singing lesson. What you heard from the Crown & Anchor Function Room was the sound of her breaking off a long-term affair.'

'I think you're wrong, Carole.'

'I see. You're the expert here on man/woman relationships, are you?'

Jude had heard her neighbour behaving like this many times before. Carole was as sensitive as if she'd had a layer of skin removed. And, of course, the fact was that Jude probably did know more about man/woman relationships. But she wasn't about to say that and launch Carole on a diatribe about her friend's chequered past.

So she said, calmly, 'Not about man/woman relationships in general, no. But I have probably had more experience of dealing with this kind of situation than you have.'

'This would be through your *healing* work, I take it?' Carole was incapable of pronouncing the word without a sneer.

'Yes,' came the patient reply. 'A lot of my clients have come to me because of relationship difficulties.'

'And have you managed to *cure* them?' Another word that always wore a layer of scepticism.

'I have been able to help some of them. Others I have referred to therapists who specialize in the relevant area.'

'So, what are you saying about Heather Mallett?'

'I am saying that, having suffered during a deeply unhappy marriage, she may have been making progress in rebuilding the social side of her life, but she still had difficulties in more . . . intimate situations. There's not only the incident with KK. In the church hall after the wedding, Bob Hinkley put his hand on her arm, and Heather recoiled like she'd been scalded. She just could not bear to be touched by a man. Something must have happened in the past that traumatized her.'

'You mean something must have happened during her marriage that traumatized her?'

Jude realized she had inadvertently got into a danger area. 'Maybe,' she replied, as if the answer wasn't important.

'Are you saying that Leonard Mallett abused his wife?'

'I'm just saying that he was obviously a difficult man to live with. I don't know any more details than that,' she lied.

'I see,' said Carole, still with a touch of doubt. 'And what about Alice? She clearly had a difficult relationship with her father. Is there any suggestion that he abused her?'

Jude hadn't been expecting Carole to get so close to the truth, and realized how inextricably she was now caught up in the web of lies. To say for a certainty that Alice had not been abused would inevitably lead to enquiries as to where she had got that information from. And Carole's Rottweiler tendency would not allow her to leave the investigation there. Soon she'd be back to questioning Alice's role in her father's death.

So, all Jude said was, 'We just don't know. It's difficult to guess what goes on inside a marriage – particularly when both husband and wife are dead.'

'Well, I think you should talk to Alice about it. She might know something about the inside of the marriage, which could have relevance to her stepmother's murder.'

Jude was very glad Carole had said 'you' rather than 'we'. She had been planning to contact Alice again, anyway, but, for many reasons, it was an interview she would rather conduct on her own.

'Yes,' she said. 'I'll talk to her.'

'Sorrento' looked less welcoming than it had on Jude's last visit. Partly, the weather was dull, and she had walked there through a cold rain, a reminder that summer had not arrived yet. Then, of course, Heather's absence, not to mention the circumstances of her departure, cast a pall over the house. Also, the place was in a state of chaos, little of which could now be blamed on the inevitable police searches. Alice appeared to have made no effort to keep the house tidy. Clothes were scattered over the furniture, and surfaces were covered with abandoned coffee cups and half-finished meals.

As she entered the sitting room, Jude made no

comment on the mess. The view of the sea was grey and despairing, matching the mood of Alice Mallett.

'No police tape around,' Jude observed. 'Have they concluded their investigations?

'God knows,' said Alice listlessly. 'They never tell me anything. Just that I should be prepared for further questioning.'

'Presumably, they've asked you about your father?' The girl nodded. 'Have they found out about the abuse?'

'I don't think so. I was questioned in exhaustive detail by two women detectives – very sensitive, clearly trained in dealing with mental health sufferers. They asked directly about abuse. I said nothing like that went on. They appeared to believe me, but who knows . . . what will happen in the "further questioning"?'

'I think you could be all right. You and Heather were the only two who knew about it, weren't you? It never got outside the family.'

'No, Dad saw to that,' said Alice grimly. 'But, of course, now *you* know.'

'I promised Heather I'd keep quiet about it. I promised you I'd keep quiet about it. And I'm not someone who goes back on their promises.'

'Thank you,' said the girl, wearily grateful.

Jude considered mentioning Carole's dangerously close interest in the situation but couldn't see how the knowledge could be of any help to Alice.

At that moment the landline rang. Alice did not even look at the phone and made no attempt to answer it. She just listened to her stepmother's answering recording and the message that followed it.

'Hi, this is Blake Woodruff. I've only just come back from a tour to Australia and heard the dreadful news about Heather. Heather Mallett, that is. I don't even know if I'm leaving this message on the right phone. It's the last number I had for her. Anyway, if Alice or some other family member picks this up, please get back to me.' He gave his mobile number. 'I'd love to know about funeral arrangements or any other details. And let me just say, I'm absolutely devastated by the news.'

'I'll ring him back,' said Alice, making no move to do anything. 'I've had so many calls like that.'

'Calls from people as famous as Blake Woodruff?'

'No, I think he was the only famous person Mum knew. I just meant that people keep leaving messages like that, and every time the answering machine clicks on, I hear her voice again, and it's like she's in the room. And that just, kind of . . .' Her eyes were glazed with tears '. . . turns the knife in the wound.'

'Mm. Just now you said your stepmother knew Blake Woodruff.'

'Yes, she did.'

'But I thought it was you who knew him. You met him through some charity fundraiser.'

'Yes, I did. But I wouldn't have got the gig if Mum hadn't pulled some strings. She contacted Blake and asked him if space could be made for me. She was doing her bit to help my stumbling career in the theatre.'

'Oh. So how long had they known each other?'

'Met in Manchester, at uni, I think. Sang in some choir together. I kind of got the impression that at one time they might have been quite close. But it was difficult to get her to talk about that kind of thing, about anything that happened before she met Dad, really.'

'Hm. Blake Woodruff's message sounded like he still meant something to her.'

'Maybe.'

'You don't know how long ago they last met?'

Alice shook her head. 'Not since she married Dad, I'm sure of that. He didn't let her see anyone – and certainly not another man.'

'No. One odd thing . . .'

'What?'

'When Blake Woodruff's name came up at a church choir rehearsal, Heather told Jonny Virgo that you were the one who knew him, not her. Why do you think she'd say that?'

Alice grimaced wryly. 'I'd imagine she wanted people to think that I'd got the gig with Blake off my own bat. She didn't want to look like she'd been calling in favours for me. She was always very protective when the subject of my career came up. She tried to cover up the fact that I hadn't really got much of a career.' This wasn't spoken with self-pity, it was just a bald statement of fact.

'Ah.' There were still some unanswered questions there, but Jude let the subject rest and moved on. 'Dare I ask if you've heard anything from Roddy?'

'Nothing.' The tears that she had managed to hold at the edge of her eyelids spilled over now.

'I was thinking . . . about the row you had on your wedding night . . . If you don't want to talk about it, of course I don't mind,' Jude lied.

'I might as well talk about it. You already know so much about my life, why should you be spared the full misery of it?'

Jude let the silence ride. If she was going to get any further confidences, she had to let the girl take her time.

Then Alice spoke. 'It's just another thing that was totally screwed up by my father. You've no idea how much he damaged me. All my relationships with men have been disastrous. I thought, with Roddy, I could finally get things right, but Dad managed to ruin that too.'

'How?'

'Look, I'm not a virgin, obviously, after my bloody father had fiddled with me for years, but . . . here's something you don't hear very often in this day and age . . . Roddy and I hadn't made love before we got married.'

Jude was surprised, but all she said was, 'Fair enough. Your choice.'

'My choice, initially. Then his choice. The fact is, we did go to bed together a few times. We tried, but on every occasion I . . . I remembered Dad touching me, and I just froze. I couldn't. Roddy and I loved each other, but I . . . couldn't.

'He was amazing about it. Must be hard for a man, any man, but particularly in this day and age. Of course, he'd never admit he wasn't having sex with me, but, particularly in a masculine world like the army, with all his mates boasting of their conquests and . . . Anyway, like I say, he was amazingly good with me, didn't put any pressure on. He kept saying it would be different when we were actually married. Once we'd got rings on our fingers, everything would turn out all right.' Alice lapsed into silence.

'But it didn't?' Jude prompted gently.

'No. Perhaps our expectations had been too high. The day of the wedding had been wonderful. We both genuinely thought we could put the past behind us, that the future was ours. And the hotel was lovely. The room was beautiful, champagne laid on. If ever there was a romantic setting, ripe for love . . . But the memory of my father was still there. At first, the kissing, the gentle kissing was . . . But when Roddy touched me, intimately . . . just like every other time . . . I recoiled. I couldn't stand it!

'And of course, it had an effect on him. Having your wife turn away from you on your wedding night . . . it doesn't do a lot for a man's potency. He couldn't, kind of . . . And suddenly, we're shouting at each other, and . . .' Alice crumpled in despair.

'And did Roddy know why you behaved like that? Had you told him about your father, about what he did to you?'

'No. I kept getting near the subject, I kept being about to tell him, but then I got scared I'd frighten him off. I thought he'd be disgusted with me when he knew what I had done with my father, for my father. I was afraid. Then, only a few hours later, I hear that Mum's been murdered.'

Again, Jude let the silence run its course, before saying, 'Roddy shouted at you, you said.'

'Mm.'
'What did he say?'
'He said it was all Mum's fault. He said that she was frigid, and the way she brought me up had made me frigid too. He said he'd had enough of her interfering in every aspect of our lives. He said he was going to sort her out, once and for all.'
The two women looked at each other bleakly. They didn't need to voice the identical thoughts which were going through both of their minds.

Eighteen

It had stopped raining by the time Jude left Sorrento for the walk back to Woodside Cottage. The capricious May weather had decided it *was* summer, after all. The sun was hot enough to raise steam from the wet paving. Fethering Beach looked breathtakingly beautiful, but Jude's mood was far from sunny. Alice's words echoed and re-echoed around her head. What she had heard had not surprised her, but it was chilling to have her worst conjectures confirmed.

As she walked along the promenade, lost in gloomy speculation, Jude became aware of a couple coming towards her. From a distance, she thought she knew who they were; the wheelchair was a giveaway. And as they got closer, she waved at Jonny Virgo and his mother. The old lady was again immaculately turned out, in her camel coat with the brown handbag clutched on her lap.

She showed no signs of recognizing Jude, but smiled benignly as Jonny greeted her.

'Weather's picked up a bit,' he began, uncontroversially.

'Certainly has.'

'An hour or so back, I didn't think we'd be able to go out all day. And Mother does so like her "turn along the prom". But . . .' He spread his hands wide '. . . lo and behold – sun!'

Though Mrs Virgo was probably not taking

anything in, Jude still felt she had to move circumspectly towards the subject that was uppermost in her mind. 'I thought the music at the wedding was wonderful, Jonny,' she said. 'You really were playing out of your skin.'

'Thank you.' He spoke modestly but was clearly delighted by the compliment.

'Terrible,' said Jude, edging towards her goal, 'that such a joyous occasion should have such a tragic outcome.'

'Yes.' Jonny Virgo looked appropriately sobered by the reminder.

'It just seems awful. Heather had come so far.'

'What do you mean?'

'The way she reinvented herself after her husband's death.'

'Ah, yes. Well, I suppose people react to bereavement in different ways. Heather was perhaps the resilient type. She recognized that one chapter of her life had closed and was moving quickly on to the next one.'

He spoke as if unaware that there had been anything wrong in the Malletts' marriage. If that's what he thought, Jude wasn't about to disillusion him. There was no reason why he should know, after all. 'You're probably right. Anyway, you won't be surprised to know that everyone in Fethering has a different theory as to the identity of Heather's murderer.'

'Oh, really? Yes, I suppose they would. I don't hear much local chat, I'm afraid. Except for these "turns along the prom", and of course my church choir commitments, Mother and I don't leave the house much.'

'Well, believe me, the Fethering gossip machine has been going into overdrive.'

'I suppose that's no surprise. Well . . .' he started the sentence as if he was about to say goodbye, but his curiosity proved too strong. 'So, who's the smart money on for the role of murderer?'

'Oh, the usual Fethering mix. Everyone who ever had any contact with Heather, even down to the milkman. Along with the customary identity parade of Russian assassins, jihadists and illegal immigrants.'

'Ah. And do you yourself have a theory, Jude?'

'Nothing worth mentioning. What about you, Jonny? If you were asked the same question, where would your finger be pointing?'

'I could only base a theory on events concerning Heather which I have personally witnessed. Which means, basically, things that I have observed during rehearsals for the church choir.'

'And . . .?'

'Well, you may remember the difficult task I had early on, when I was sorting out who would actually be singing at the wedding . . .?'

Jude caught on quickly. 'And you told Ruskin Dewitt he couldn't be part of the choir on the big day.'

'Exactly. Then, when he appealed to the rest of the choir to make me change my mind, who was it who backed me up strongly, and said she didn't think he was good enough to sing at the wedding?'

'Heather.'

'Yes. And she expressed her views quite forcibly. Listen, Russ and I go back a long way. I've known him on and off for years. Apart from anything else, we taught at the same school, Ravenhall, for more than a decade. So, I know his character pretty well.'

'And . . .?' Jude repeated.

'And . . . beneath his surface bonhomie, Russ has a very violent streak.'

'Oh?'

'He keeps it under control most of the time, but occasionally it just bursts out. He's capable of turning very nasty. At the school where we both taught, he nearly lost his job once for assaulting a pupil.'

'When you say, "assaulting", do you mean "sexually assaulting"?'

'Oh, good heavens, no!' Jonny coloured. 'Nothing like that ever happened at Ravenhall. And I can't imagine Russ being involved in that kind of disgusting stuff. No, he just lost his rag with the kid and lashed out. He does have a ferocious temper on him, and he's also the kind of person who holds grudges for a very long time.'

'But do you mean that he'd been nursing a grievance about what Heather said to—?'

'Better be off now, Jude.' He unclicked the brakes on the wheelchair. 'As it is, I've probably said more than I should. See you soon. Say goodbye, Mother.'

'Goodbye,' said Mrs Virgo obediently and serenely. Though who she was saying it to, she had no idea.

Jude was frustrated when she got back to Woodside Cottage. Jonny Virgo's suspicion of

Ruskin Dewitt was just a diversion. The main track of guilt she was following led directly to Roddy Skelton. And to no one else.

Her frustration arose from her inability to progress in finding the missing bridegroom. Still, there was one thing she could try. And any action was better than none. She picked up the local telephone directory. Nothing wrong with going for the obvious first.

The copy of the telephone directory she had was an old one. She knew that a lot of such listings were now done online. But at least the phonebook she had would list people who'd been at their addresses for some time.

There were only two Skeltons listed. 'Skelton, A. W.' and 'Skelton, P.', one in Angmering, one in Smalting. She rang the latter and was excited by the voice which spelled out his number at the other end. The elderly voice of a man who had been to the right schools, but who was now in a state of high tension. She felt sure it was the tall man she'd seen in All Saints for the wedding.

'Good morning. Is that Mr Skelton?'

'Yes.'

'Are you the father of Roddy Skelton?'

'Yes. Why, do you know where he is?' The patrician voice dropped to a tone of agonized pleading.

'No, I'm sorry, I don't.'

'Ah.' The pain was now of disappointment.

'Listen, my name's Jude.'

'Are you the Jude who lives in Fethering and works as a healer?'

'Yes, I am. Why, have we met?'

'No. No, we haven't. It's just that a very good friend of mine took advantage of your services when he developed a back problem immediately after he retired. He spoke very highly of you. You got him back on the golf course, where he has developed an unfortunate habit of beating me on a weekly basis.'

'Are we talking about . . .?' and she mentioned a name.

'That's the fellow. He said you were very good. It had never occurred to him that the pain was in his mind. And I must say the idea sounds pretty fanciful to me. Any pain I've ever felt has been in my body. But my pal's a hundred per cent better, so I guess the proof of the pudding . . .'

'The mind and the body are inseparable. It's inevitable that a major trauma like retirement is going to have some effect on a person. It's just a question of what form that effect takes.'

'Yes.' The sharpness of the response did not suggest Mr Skelton was convinced by such views. 'Anyway, he's extremely grateful to you. Said he'd recommend you to anyone who's got problems in the . . . you know, in the mind department.' For a moment, he sounded exactly like his son. He spoke with the bluff certainty of someone who would never himself admit to having 'problems in the mind department'.

'The reason I'm ringing,' said Jude, 'is that I'm a friend of Alice Mallett.' She didn't think that was overstating the case.

'Ah. Needless to say, she's rung me many times

since Roddy disappeared. But neither of us is any closer to finding out what's happened to him.'

'Presumably the police have been in touch with you?'

'And how? Though they haven't put it into words, it's pretty clear that they think he was responsible for Heather Mallett's death. Which I just cannot believe. I know he suffered a lot of stress when he was out in Afghanistan, and it sometimes makes him do irrational things, but I really cannot think of my son as a murderer.'

'I fully understand that. And, having met him, I can't think of Roddy as a murderer either. I'm sure soon the police will find out who did actually kill Heather.'

'But will they find Roddy?' There was despair in the voice now. 'I'm so worried about him.'

'You've presumably checked with his friends? The best man, for instance? He's not holing up with any of them?'

'No, I've checked. So have the police. There's no sign of him anywhere.'

'Well, look, if I hear anything, I'll get back to you.'

'Thank you.' Fortunately, the old man was so concerned to hear news of his son that he didn't think to ask what possible reason Jude had for being part of the hunt.

'And, Mr Skelton, if you could let me know if you hear anything . . .?'

'Yes, of course.'

She gave him her mobile number. 'I'm sure you'll hear good news about Roddy soon.'

'Yes. Thank you. I'm sure I will.' But the old voice didn't sound optimistic.

Jude bit the bullet and went round to High Tor. She knew that, when Carole sensed some estrangement between them, Jude would always have to be the one who set about mending the fences. She also knew that keeping the identity of Leonard Mallett's murderer from her neighbour wasn't going to get any easier.

It was characteristic of Carole that she made no mention of their latest brief estrangement, but immediately invited her friend in for a cup of coffee. And, rather than voicing suspicions of Alice, she went straight into a re-creation of her encounter with KK Rosser. Jude listened with interest but made no comment when told about Heather Mallett's recoil from the guitarist's touch. That was moving too close to the subject of Leonard Mallett's abusive habits.

She then gave Carole an edited version of her own investigative achievements over the last few days. She didn't pass on Alice's account of their wedding night, but did tell of Roddy's disappearance and the telephone conversation she had had with his father.

'Where do you think he's gone?' asked Carole.

'No idea. But nothing's really going to happen on the case until he's found.'

'He's presumably the police's Number One Suspect?'

'He may be. They have kept their customary discreet silence on the matter. They're certainly not about to share their thinking with us. But the coincidence of Heather's death and Roddy's disappearance does look at least suspicious.'

'Yes. And do we have any other suspects?'

'The usual Fethering line-up. Oh, and another one we can add to the list, as of this morning.'

'Who's that?'

And Jude told Carole what Jonny Virgo had said to her on the promenade only a few hours before.

'Ruskin Dewitt? Really? Well, that is interesting. I did see him lose his temper quite dramatically at one of the Preservation of Fethering's Seafront committee meetings.' She looked thoughtful. 'I'm aware that he didn't recognize me last time we met, but, you know, I think I might have a word with Ruskin Dewitt.'

That was fine by Jude. She did not for a moment believe that the retired schoolteacher had anything to do with Heather Mallett's death. But if Carole concentrated on him, it would at least prevent her from poking her nose into other, more sensitive areas of the investigation.

Nineteen

Carole also tried the direct approach. She rang Ruskin Dewitt and said she wanted to talk to him about Heather Mallett's death. He welcomed the idea enthusiastically. 'I have felt rather out of the loop up here in Fedborough, and then I've been away,' he said, 'missing all the gossip which I am sure is swamping Fethering like a tsunami.'

Carole confirmed that the village had indeed been full of criminal conjecture.

His house was one of those neat little Victorian cottages by what used to be the Fedborough Wharf on the River Fether. They were still sometimes referred to as 'workmen's cottages', which was rather ridiculous, given the amount of renovation they had undergone, and the prices they now commanded.

The interior was tiny. The book-lined study into which he ushered her had an attractive view, through small wood-framed panes, on to the river. Carole didn't know whether Ruskin had ever been married, or was a widower, but she thought the place lacked a woman's touch. She respected tidiness, but she didn't feel even High Tor boasted this same level of military precision in the way the bookshelves were stacked and the furniture aligned. On one table, she noticed, was a regimented pile of guidebooks to the Holy Land.

She accepted his offer of coffee, and the efficiency with which he produced it also suggested someone who was used to fending for himself. While occupied in the adjacent tiny kitchen, he kept up a monologue, describing his life in Fedborough. She hadn't asked for the information, but she got the impression that anyone who visited him would be subjected to the same litany.

'I'm very involved locally,' he said. 'On the committee of the Fedborough Museum; was very instrumental in all of the fundraising when we moved it from the High Street premises to the riverside. And I'm getting increasingly busy doing stuff for the church. All Souls it is – not to be confused with All Saints in Fethering. As you know, I used to go there, but I find the Fedborough set-up more congenial. More High Church, apart from anything else, and I've always had a natural tendency in that direction. Even considered converting to Catholicism at one point, but decided against. Found transubstantiation a bit of a stumbling block. Anyway, I'm involved at All Souls as a sidesman – and in the choir, of course, and in the Friends of All Souls' fundraising activities. Then, there's the Local History Society . . .'

As he went on, Carole recognized, from her own experience, what Ruskin Dewitt's secret was. He was lonely, desperately lonely. That was why he had so avidly to fill his time. He didn't dare to be alone for a moment. That was, without doubt, why he had agreed so readily to see her. Any human contact was preferable to being on his own.

When they were settled with their coffees in a pair of chintz-covered campaign chairs either side of the window, Carole used the opportunity of Ruskin Dewitt taking a breath to interpolate, 'As we discussed on the phone, Fethering is a hotbed of gossip about Heather Mallett's death.'

'I'm sure it is.' He rubbed his hands together. 'Right, give me all the dirt.'

'I'm not sure there is much real dirt. Plenty of speculation, of course.'

'Yes.'

'But I was just wondering whether you had seen Heather Mallett, you know, since that last choir rehearsal you went to?'

'Oh, I know when you mean. It was just round that time that I was deciding I really did prefer the All Souls style of worship to that of All Saints. So, it did turn out to be my last rehearsal in Fethering, as it happened. And, of course, resigning from the All Saints choir did cut down on the driving, particularly at night. I'm afraid the old eyesight isn't so good after dark these days; the oncoming headlights are so bright. Do you find that?'

'Not yet,' said Carole with some asperity. She didn't like being bracketed in the same age group as him. He had a good twenty years on her.

At the same time, she was mildly amused by the narrative that Ruskin Dewitt had created to explain his leaving the All Saints choir. Now it was being presented as a considered decision, nothing to do with his being banned from singing at Alice Mallett's wedding. From the confident way he spoke of it, Carole felt sure he now regarded his version of events as the truth.

'But had you seen Heather since that rehearsal?' she asked.

'No. No reason why I should. I didn't know her outside the choir.'

'Of course not.' Carole trod delicately. 'I wasn't at that rehearsal . . .'

'You wouldn't have been.'

'No, I regret that choirs are not for me. Tone deaf, I'm afraid.' She could never resist saying that when the subject came up.

'Your loss, Carole. I don't know where I'd be without my choral singing. Been doing it all my adult life. I find singing with other people is a wonderful emotional release.'

Even if you're always out of tune, thought Carole uncharitably. 'And do you find you have a lot of emotion to release?'

'What do you mean?' His affronted response made her realize how clumsy her change of direction had been. Jude, she felt sure, would have done it better.

She tried to lighten the atmosphere by saying, 'I just meant, we're all up against the frustrations of daily life, aren't we? The continual stresses of disturbing news bulletins, the general state of chaos that seems to be everywhere in today's world. I'm sure we all need some means of, I don't know . . . counteracting that stress. You're lucky that choral singing does it for you.'

'Yes, I suppose I am,' he said, somewhat mollified. 'And what is your means of release, Carole?'

'I beg your pardon?'

'What do you do to stop yourself from being uptight all the time?'

She wondered, for a moment, if he was making a joke. She knew a lot of people in Fethering would be of the view that she was 'uptight all the time'. But she countered the insinuation with an airy, 'Oh, I find a walk with my dog on Fethering Beach usually sorts me out.'

The statement wasn't true, but he didn't seem interested enough to challenge it. Instead he said, 'Talking of Fethering Beach . . . you haven't heard any talk of reviving the Preservation of Fethering's Seafront committee since Leonard Mallett died, have you?'

'I haven't heard anything, no.'

'It was a good initiative, but like all these things, it needs someone dynamic and proactive to make anything happen. I considered reviving it myself but, quite honestly, I'm so busy with the various other committees I'm on . . . and the church, of course. Leonard's set-up was trying to get local people to form a rota of clearing plastic from the beach, that kind of thing.'

'I know,' said Carole icily. 'I was actually on the committee.'

'Were you?' He looked at her in amazement, before saying, 'Oh yes, of course you were.'

She didn't now think his earlier lack of recognition was caused by failing memory or rudeness. She had come to the conclusion that Ruskin Dewitt was just one of those men who was so involved in his own ego, that he really didn't notice other people.

Carole moved her investigation forward. 'I

gather that you and Jonny Virgo taught at the same school for a while.'

'Yes. Ravenhall. For our sins.' He let out the meaningless laugh that always accompanies that meaningless expression.

'And did you get on well?' Again, it was a very direct question, but Carole reckoned Russ was so caught up in himself that, so long as the conversation centred on him, he didn't mind too much what he was being asked.

Her instinct proved right. 'Well, we sort of rubbed along, as you do in a school staff room. We're very different people, though. I was always more active, setting up new initiatives for the sixth formers, that kind of thing. Jonny had less natural empathy with the boys. Only really interested in his own music. And his mother, even back then. Devoted to her. Bit of an "apron strings problem", but he's always had that.'

'And did you ever have any trouble at the school?'

'Me? Why should I have trouble?'

'I gather you sometimes had a problem with controlling your temper.'

That really did catch him on the raw. 'I have never in my life had problems controlling my temper!' he bellowed in a voice which immediately gave the lie to what he was saying. 'And if someone has been spreading rumours about me, I demand to know who it is! What have you heard?'

'Just that you once lost your temper so badly that you assaulted one of the pupils.'

'That is a downright lie!' Quickly deciding that

bluster was not going to be his best way out of this situation, he took on a more conciliatory tone. 'Oh, I think I probably know the incident you are referring to. And I bet you heard it from bloody Jonny, didn't you?'

Carole neither confirmed nor denied this.

'Very well, I'll tell you exactly what happened. Yes, one of the boys did accuse me of hitting him, I don't deny that. But the fact was that the boy in question was a fantasist. He was from a very unsettled background – his parents were going through a sticky divorce at the time – and the boy expressed his mental turmoil by spreading mendacious rumours about his classmates. Presumably getting some kind of kick out of this, he decided to move up the food chain and spread a rumour about a member of staff. I got the short straw of being the one he chose. The boy said I had hit him over the head with a dictionary.

'The headmaster of Ravenhall at the time was not very bright, but he knew what was required of him in such circumstances. Very rightly, he took the accusation that had been made against me seriously. And it's always difficult in such situations to be certain of the truth. It was basically the boy's version of events against mine. Fortunately, in the end, wiser counsel prevailed, and I was exonerated. I agreed not to seek any apology, or indeed to ask that the boy should be punished. It was an unsavoury incident, but one that is a hazard of choosing schoolmastering as one's profession. I imagine the risks of such unwarranted accusations are even greater now in the days of social media. At least, thank goodness, I was spared that.

'But even though I was completely cleared by the in-school enquiry, the fact that Jonny Virgo still remembers the incident shows just how firmly mud sticks.'

Carole couldn't be certain, but she suspected that Russ's explanation of this incident had as much relation to the truth as his narrative of why he left the Fethering church choir. He had the skill of finessing history into a version that he found acceptable. That did not mean, though, that he didn't believe it.

Anyway, the demonstration of his temper was not going to deflect Carole from the course on which she had set out. 'Going back to the question of whether you'd seen Heather Mallett since you left the All Saints choir . . .'

'I've already answered that. I . . .' He stopped himself, and a new knowingness came into his eyes. 'Oh, I see. The amateur sleuths of Fethering have been putting their heads together, haven't they? Examining the evidence, and coming up with their solution to the whodunit mystery? And I am being honoured with the role of perpetrator, am I?'

'No. There is just a natural concern about—'

'Natural concern my foot! Natural nosiness more likely! Natural suspicion of the outsider, of anyone who doesn't fit the box of neatly married conformist!'

His anger was revealing more of his self-image than he probably wanted to give away. Carole found it interesting that both Ruskin Dewitt and

KK Rosser, coming from such different directions, shared contempt for the safely married archetype.

'I've had to put up with this kind of discrimination right through my life,' he went on, 'particularly when I was teaching. Why can't people understand that there are some of us who are self-sufficient, who just get on with things, who don't need to be part of some bloody community?'

Though Russ wasn't, Carole was aware of the contradictions in what he was saying. His claim to self-sufficiency was nonsense; rarely had she encountered someone who seemed more desperate to be part of a community, any community. He was one of those deluded individuals who saw himself as the life and soul of the parties he never got invited to.

But she didn't say anything. She couldn't say anything. Ruskin Dewitt was in full flow.

'Well, in this case, you can gossip as much as you like, but you'll never pin the crime on me. Heather Mallett was murdered last weekend, right?'

'Yes. After her stepdaughter's wedding.'

'And do you know where I was last weekend?' He rose suddenly from his campaign chair and picked up the neat pile of guidebooks. 'Have you ever been to the Holy Land, Carole?'

'No.'

'Maybe you should try it. Concentrating on spiritual matters might possibly cure that nasty suspicious mind of yours. It's a very inspiring place, you know, the Holy Land. I helped to organize a trip there for the Friends of All Souls Fedborough. A trip from which we only returned on Monday. So, at the time when Heather Mallett was strangled, sixteen High Church Christians from Fedborough can vouch for the fact that I was in a hotel near the Mount of Olives.' He grinned without humour. 'Well, Carole, would you like to withdraw your unfounded accusation?'

'I'm sorry,' she mumbled.

'I'm glad to hear it. I think, in the circumstances, it would not be appropriate for me to offer you any more coffee.'

'No, probably not.' She picked up her handbag and rose from her chair. In the small space, Ruskin Dewitt seemed to loom over her. 'I'll be on my way then,' she mumbled.

He stood back to let her pass. But he didn't stand back far enough to cease to be threatening. As she got to the front door, his voice arrested her. 'Would you like to know where I think you should look for Heather's murderer?'

'I'd be very interested, yes.'

'I'm sure you would. And what would you say are the usual motives for murder?'

Carole stayed silent. He might want to play games. She didn't.

'Sex, financial gain, fear of exposure. I reckon that covers most of them. You know, for a long time, until I decided to give it up, I sang with the church choir of All Saints Fethering.'

'I know you did.' She didn't like being toyed with. She wanted just to walk out. But, on the other hand, if he did actually have a useful suggestion for where she should next direct her investigation . . .

'So, I know the individuals involved pretty well. Given their age and character, I think we can forget the motivations of sex and financial gain. But fear of exposure . . .'

'You mean, having a secret that you don't want to have exposed . . .?'

'That's exactly what I mean. So, which of the All Saints choir members do you think might have such a secret?'

'I don't know all of them.'

'But, come on, Carole, you know who they *are*. You live in Fethering, for God's sake. Everyone there knows who everyone else *is*.' She didn't argue. 'Who's concealing what then? Could it be that Shirley and Veronica Tattersall are incestuous lesbians . . .?'

'If you're just going to be stupid, I'll—'

'No, don't go. I know you don't want to . . . till you've heard my suspicions.' Once again, he was right. 'So, let's ask ourselves, who might have a secret that Heather could have found out about, a secret so shaming that he or she would resort to murder to prevent it from being disclosed?'

'Jonny Virgo?'

Ruskin Dewitt chuckled. 'No. No, much as I would like to have my revenge on the little creep for fingering me, I'm afraid that just wouldn't stack up. Jonny's made a kind of fetish of keeping his nose clean. No dirt clings to Jonny. Come on, Carole, who else?'

'As I said, I don't know them very well.'

'What's that old saying . . .?' He was clearly having fun teasing out his narrative. '"It's the quiet ones you have to watch." Now who would you say was the quietest member of that church choir?'

'I don't know . . . unless it's that woman with dyed red hair.'

'Ah,' said Ruskin Dewitt, 'now you're talking. Yes, Elizabeth Browning.'

'So, what was her secret?' asked Carole. 'The one Heather found out about?'

And he told her.

Twenty

It was worth having a look, thought Carole, as she navigated the Renault, well within the speed limit, back to Fethering.

She put the car in the High Tor garage and walked down towards the Fethering Yacht Club. The weather had now turned almost summery. The Seaview Café, which opened out on to the beach, had, for the first time that year, put some tables and chairs outside.

And another denizen of Fethering had returned to summer habits. As Carole rounded the side of the Fethering Yacht Club, the sea wall which contained the ferocious flow of the River Fether was revealed. And, leaning against it, looking out to sea, was Elizabeth Browning.

In the sunlight, the colour of her long hair looked even less natural. And her French Lieutenant's Woman pose looked even more affected.

Before going up to the woman, Carole paused for a moment. It struck her that she was quite possibly now at the scene of Heather Mallett's murder. The body had certainly gone into the river, to return within only a few hours as a 'Fethering Floater'. Was it not likely that the confrontation which ended with her strangling had taken place right here, conveniently close to the sea wall?

But she didn't let this thought change her plans.

In fact, it gave her an idea for an opening gambit. She walked towards Elizabeth Browning. (In normal Fethering resident mode, Carole would never have gone straight up to someone to whom she hadn't been properly introduced. But Carole in investigative mode was a totally different creature. Her interest in murder had done a lot for her social skills, helping to overcome her natural shyness.)

'Good morning, Elizabeth,' she said.

The woman turned and squinted, trying to identify the outline against the bright sunshine.

'Carole Seddon. We've met at the Crown & Anchor a few times.' Well, once, anyway. And then we didn't actually address a word to each other. But never mind, there are questions I want to ask you.

'Oh yes. Good morning,' said Elizabeth vaguely.

'Looking at the river, it's hard not to think about Heather Mallett, isn't it?' asked Carole.

But her opening gambit failed to produce any very significant reaction. 'I suppose so, perhaps.' Elizabeth Browning's mind had clearly been on anything other than the murder victim.

'Did you know her well?' Carole pressed on.

The woman shrugged. Close to, Carole could see that her make-up was very skilfully and meticulously done. It took a good ten years off her real age. 'Well, we sang in the church choir together for some years. But Heather was very buttoned-up and quiet. She wasn't the kind of person you bonded with. Turned up for rehearsals and then left, no socializing. She did relax a bit after her husband died, but I still didn't get close to her.'

'Did you ever meet her husband?' Carole was determined to investigate any links Elizabeth Browning might have to the Mallett family.

'Not meet, really, no. I saw him sometimes. On a few occasions he'd pick Heather up after rehearsal, but he always stayed waiting in the car, didn't come into the church. He and I never spoke to each other.'

'Ah.' Carole gestured towards a bench, commemorating some long-gone Fethering resident, who 'enjoyed his afternoons here looking at the sea.' 'Would you like to sit?'

Elizabeth shrugged again. The movement suggested she'd rather stay by the sea wall, but wasn't going to make a fuss about something so trivial. Perhaps she was curious as to why she had been accosted by someone she hardly knew. Or, according to Carole's more sinister interpretation, perhaps she wanted to assess how much her interrogator knew.

But it was Elizabeth who began this latest round of questioning. 'You're not married, are you, Carole?'

'Divorced,' came the short reply. She didn't really see that her marital status was anyone's business but her own.

'And you and Jude . . . you're not an item, are you?'

'Certainly not.' In spite of the sunshine, the temperature suddenly dropped.

'Sorry. But you know how rumours spread in a place like Fethering.'

'I do indeed. But that is one that, I can tell you, should be permanently scotched. Isn't it possible, in this day and age, for two women to be friends, without anything else being involved?' Carole realized she was perhaps protesting too much.

Elizabeth Browning was unruffled. 'Sure, I'm cool with that. Mind you, I'd be cool with the two of you being a couple. I think there's far too much emphasis on gender identity these days. Let people do what they want to do.'

There was an almost hippyish laissez-faire tone in her voice. Carole, becoming intrigued by the woman's personality, found herself asking, 'What about you? Are you married?'

'No. Never found a man I liked that much.' Carole had expected the answer to be self-pitying, but Elizabeth seemed very much in control, relishing her single freedom. 'And I've road-tested a few along the way,' she added.

She looked directly at Carole for the first time. Her eyes were of a brown so dark as almost to be black, hinting perhaps at a heritage from the Mediterranean – or even further east. 'Anyway, what's this about?'

'Sorry?'

'Carole, we don't really know each other. Yet you have deliberately sought me out and initiated a conversation with me. Why?'

'Well—'

'And immediately started talking about Heather Mallett's death. So, what are you doing – working through the list of murder suspects?' This was so uncomfortably close to the truth that, for a moment, Carole was silent. 'What do you want to know? Where was I on the night of the seventeenth, the evening of the wedding?'

Aware that the initiative had been taken away from her, Carole changed the line of attack. 'I've just come from talking to Ruskin Dewitt.'

'Have you? On the premise that his public humiliation by Heather about singing at the wedding was sufficient motive for him to have strangled her?'

Carole, surprised by how forceful her adversary was, tried to regain ground. 'Ruskin Dewitt couldn't have had any involvement in the crime. He was in the Holy Land last weekend.'

'Lucky Holy Land,' said Elizabeth drily. 'How much he must have added, by his mere presence, to their national well-being. But Russ, no doubt, had some dirt to spread about me, which is why I have the pleasure of your company this bright and sunny morning?'

'He did mention one or two things.'

'I'm sure he did. And he no doubt suggested that Heather had somehow found out what that dirt was, and confronted me with it. And that I had been so appalled by the thought of my secrets being spread to the world that I strangled her. Was that the way Russ's thoughts – and yours – were inclining?'

'Well . . .' Again, so uncomfortably close to the truth that Carole was lost for words.

'Right, so shall I guess what this famous "dirt" was. My terrible secret, whose exposure would shame me before the entire world? Was part of it the fact that, in spite of constantly going on about my career there, my only appearance at Glyndebourne was when some kids from local primary schools were drafted in to sing "The

Children's Chorus" in a production of *Carmen*. Is that part of what Russ told you?'

Carole was forced to admit that it was.

'If that's the case, then I've no doubt about the rest of his revelations. That I never worked professionally as a singer. That I never had a problem with nodules on my vocal chords, which cut short that promising career. That I was basically a fraud. Was that the . . . burden of his message?'

Again, there was no escaping a yes.

'Good. I'm glad we've got that straight. Well, Carole, I've owned up to you readily enough, haven't I?'

'Yes. Yes, you have.'

'So, do you really believe that keeping people from knowing about my small imposture is sufficient motive for me to kill someone?'

'It does sound unlikely.'

'It sounds more than unlikely. It sounds impossible. So, may I now perhaps be allowed to resume my morning routine of gazing wistfully out to sea?'

'Yes. But can I just ask you one thing?'

'What?'

'Why do you do it?'

'Gaze wistfully out to sea?'

'Well, that too, but I really meant why do you build up this tissue of lies about yourself, all that Glyndebourne stuff, the nodules . . .?'

'I do it, Carole, for the same reason you do it.'

'What do you mean?'

'To retain my privacy as a human being. To resist the curiosity of others.'

'Sorry?'

'You haven't been in the choir, so you wouldn't know, but I can assure you that none of the other members have ever asked me any personal questions. I've overheard them saying, "Oh, don't for heaven's sake, don't get Elizabeth going. Don't ask her anything, or you'll get the full routine about her having been a rising star at Glyndebourne, until nodules on her vocal chords cut her career tragically short."' The woman spread her hands wide with satisfaction. 'And in that way, I retain my privacy.'

'I see.'

'Except, of course, I do apparently run the risk of people coming up to me out of the blue and accusing me of murder.'

'I'm sorry, I—'

'Oh, no worries. That doesn't offend me. Amuses me, if anything. Also, brings home to me how wrong people can be.'

'What do you mean?'

'Well, if you're looking for rifts between Heather Mallett and other choir members, both in the church one and the pub one, by focusing your firepower on me, you are – if you will forgive the mixed metaphor – barking up a completely wrong tree.'

'You mean there's another tree I should be barking up?' Elizabeth just smiled at her, infuriatingly. 'Who? Who didn't Heather get on with?'

'Just a word to the wise . . . It's often the case, in a set-up like a choir, that the people who ruffle most feathers are the newest arrivals.'

'Newest arrivals? Are you talking about Jude?'

'No, of course I'm not talking about Jude.'

'Then who?'

'Ask yourself . . .' Elizabeth seemed to be having fun, playing with Carole now, 'who is the most recent arrival in Fethering?'

'Bet Harrison. Are you saying that Bet Harrison was at odds with Heather?'

'Oh, well done. Eventually you got there.' Elizabeth Browning made a skittish little clapping movement with her hands. 'But you didn't hear it from me.' She looked out towards the English Channel. 'Mm, I think I should be getting on with my busy task of looking out over the sea.'

'Just a minute . . .'

'What?'

Hesitantly, Carole asked, 'When you talked about the elaborate way in which you protect your privacy, you said I do something similar – what on earth did you mean by that?'

Elizabeth Browning positively grinned. 'Oh, come on, Carole. I've seen you around Fethering for years, always walking briskly, busy, busy, busy. Rushing from one thing you have to do to the next. Walking that dog of yours on the beach, always with a firm destination in mind, never daring to stop. I know enough about the symptoms to recognize loneliness when I see it, Carole.'

No words could provide a proper response to this devastatingly accurate analysis. But, as Elizabeth moved towards the sea wall, Carole managed to ask, 'And that, the gazing out to sea, why do you do that? Are you mourning a lost love? Or is that just another act?'

'It's a kind of act, maybe,' came the reply. 'But also, I do love looking at the sea. It's like looking at a fire, constantly changing, constantly making new patterns, constantly destroying them and reshaping the pieces. I like that. I find it very soothing.

'Also,' she added, 'you'd be surprised. Out here by the sea wall is, actually, quite a good place to pick up men.'

And she moved back into her tragic French Lieutenant's Woman pose, looking out over the unforgiving sea. Once again, thought Carole, remembering the words of Ruskin Dewitt, a reminder that it's the quiet ones you have to watch.

It was later the same day that Jude answered the telephone in Woodside Cottage.

'Good afternoon,' said the familiar regimental voice. 'This is Brian Skelton here. Roddy's father.'

'Oh, hello.'

'Listen, I hope you don't mind my asking you this – and please say no if it's inconvenient . . .'

'What is it?'

'Roddy's come back. I said I'd let you know if anything happened . . . and he's come back.'

'That's really good news.'

'Yes.' Brian Skelton didn't sound totally convinced.

'Why, what's happened? Have you told the police he's back?'

'Of course. They've been questioning him ever since I told them he was here. They've only just finished with him.'

'And . . .?' asked Jude. 'They haven't arrested him?'

'No.'

'That's good.'

'Yes.' Again, without complete conviction.

'Did they actually say they'd eliminated him from their enquiries?'

'Nothing as definite as that. In fact, they implied that they would need to question him further.' The old man sounded very weary, uncertain how much more he could take. 'Roddy's in a bad way, Jude.'

'Physically?'

'A few scratches. Nothing that won't heal. But it's more the other aspect . . .'

'His mental health?'

'I suppose we have to call it that.' It was said with the unwillingness of someone who had never in his life spoken of such matters.

'Would it help if I were to come and see him?'

'That's what I was going to ask. I know it's a cheek, but after what you did for my golfing buddy . . .'

'I'll be there as soon as I can.'

Twenty-One

Smalting was along the coast to the west of Fethering. Its residents thought of it as the more upmarket of the two villages. The residents of Fethering thought the reverse, but on the objective valuations of estate agents, prices in Smalting were marginally higher. Which explained the air of smugness worn by many of the locals.

The house in which Brian Skelton lived was small and neat, with probably, Jude judged from the exterior, only two bedrooms. She got the feeling that, when Roddy had been young and meeting Alice at the Fethering Yacht Club, the family would have lived in a bigger property. Whether the downsizing had occurred before or after the death of Mrs Skelton, she did not know. She dismissed her taxi driver. It was a Fethering-based firm she used often, and she said she might call him back for the return trip.

The man who opened the front door to her was, as she had expected, the man she'd seen at the wedding. Tall and wiry, with white hair and fiercely black brows over pure blue eyes. Brian Skelton was slightly stooped with age, but still looked capable of a completing a couple of rounds of golf a week.

'It's good of you to come,' he said.

'No problem.'

'Roddy's very low.' As he ushered her into the

small, anonymous hall, he asked, 'Can I get you a coffee or . . .?'

'No, thanks. I had some just before I left.'

'He's hardly talking to me. I don't know if you'll be able to get anything out of him.'

'We'll see. Is he in bed?'

'No. In the sitting room at the back.'

'Does he know I'm coming?'

'I said you were. Whether he took it in . . .' He shrugged.

'Let's go and see him.'

'Yes. Do you want me to . . . er . . .?' he asked awkwardly.

'I think if you're around when I first talk to him . . . then we'll play it by ear.'

'Fine.' Still, he didn't move towards the back of the house. 'It is terrible for me, seeing my son in this condition. He was pretty shaken each time he came back from Afghanistan, but nothing like this.'

'He's probably reacting to the accumulated stress.'

'Perhaps. I was a career soldier too, but we never had . . . Attitudes were different. I don't know, perhaps we weren't subjected to the same pressures. Certainly, we never talked about stuff like that.'

'And do you think that was a good thing?' asked Jude gently.

The blue eyes looked piercingly into her brown ones. 'I don't know. Sometimes I do, sometimes I don't.'

'Let's go and see Roddy.'

'Yes.'

The small sitting room opened on to a conservatory which caught the afternoon sunshine. Like the hall, it was furnished efficiently rather than affectionately. The only personal touches were family photographs, Roddy and a sister at various ages in various seaside and boating situations. There was no photographic evidence of the late Mrs Skelton. On the small table beside the armchair in which Roddy sat was a framed picture of him in his full uniformed glory, probably taken at his Sandhurst passing-out ceremony.

The contrast between the beaming young man in the photograph and the figure who shrank into the armchair beside it could not have been more marked. Though their bulk was much the same. At the end of his Sandhurst training, Roddy had been at the peak of his physical fitness. In the years since he had put on enough weight to become almost chubby. But whatever he had been doing since the previous Saturday had stripped him of those excess pounds. He looked thin, gaunt, haunted. The jogging suit he wore hung loose on his frame. Though the scratches and bruises on his face had been cleaned up, they still looked livid and painful. His eyes were open, but unfocused.

'Roddy,' she said gently. 'It's Jude. Do you remember me?'

He showed no signs of recognition. No signs of hearing her. He seemed locked into his own silence.

'This is pretty much how he was when he arrived here,' said his father. 'Filthy dirty, scratched all over. I cleaned him up. He didn't say much.'

'Did he come here of his own accord?'

'I think so. Nobody drove him, if that's what you mean. Just a couple of days ago, there was a knock on the front door, and there he was.'

'I think that's a good sign, that he knew where to come back to.'

'Maybe,' said the old man, in the manner of someone who had clutched at so many straws recently that he wasn't much excited by being offered a new one.

'And you say he did talk to the police?'

'Yes. They didn't want me to be there while they questioned him, but I could hear his voice from the kitchen. He was definitely talking to them.'

'And did he tell you where he'd been since he left the Craigmullen?'

'He sort of implied he'd been on the Downs. He used to spend a lot of time out there when he was a boy, and his training taught him basic fieldcraft, so he wouldn't have had a problem surviving.'

'And those wounds on his face – was he attacked by someone?'

'I don't know for sure, but I think they're probably just scratches from brambles and what-have-you.'

'Hm.' Gently, Jude took the young man's hand. 'Roddy. Can you hear me, Roddy?' There was no reaction.

'My instinct,' said Brian Skelton, 'is just to tell him to snap out of it.'

'I don't think that's a good idea, Mr Skelton. Your son is seriously ill.'

'Mentally ill?'

'Yes.'

The old man groaned. He was out of his depth in such talk. 'I just never imagined . . . He was always such a happy child, full of enthusiasm for everything. And he loves the army. All right, he's probably seen some pretty nasty stuff at times, Afghanistan certainly, but he's basically always been as sane as I am.'

Jude didn't comment. She wasn't about to challenge Brian Skelton's lifetime disbelief in the existence of mental illness. Instead, she said, 'If you wouldn't mind, I'd like to spend some time with Roddy on his own . . .?'

'Yes, yes, of course. Absolutely fine. I'll go and . . . er . . . make myself a cup of coffee. Get you one?'

'No thank you, I'm fine.'

'Oh yes, you said. Good, excellent. Well, I'll . . . erm . . .' And he shuffled awkwardly out of the room, closing the door behind him.

'Roddy . . .' Jude kept her voice very low. 'I'm just going to try a healing technique that will relax you. It doesn't involve my actually touching you, but . . .'

She stopped, because she suddenly noticed that a spark of life had come into his eyes.

'Sorry,' he said. 'I just can't talk when the Aged P is in the room. I know I've let everyone down, but I've let him down most of all.'

'In what way?'

'He always wanted me to be a son he could be proud of. That's why I went into the army. To please him. And I've let him down. He wanted a son who could cope with life, not a bloody basket case.' Unbidden, tears were now trickling down his scratched cheeks. 'Oh God, and now I'm blubbing like a new bug on his first day at prep school. Thank God the Aged P isn't in the room to witness this!'

'Roddy, don't worry about it. Listen, you're seriously ill.'

'Ill? Sick in the head. Unable to hack it. The Aged P wouldn't regard that as a proper illness.'

'In this case, his opinion doesn't matter. I've had some medical training . . .' (She didn't mention the fact that some people, like Carole, would not regard the courses she had undergone as *proper* medical training.) '. . . and I'm telling you you're ill.'

'Finished,' he said despairingly. 'Come to the end of the road.'

'No, Roddy. You've got a lot more road to travel.'

'I don't think I can face it. I want it all to end. I can't take any more.'

'What did you do,' asked Jude softly, 'after you left Alice at the Craigmullen last Saturday night?'

'I drove up into the Downs. There's an abandoned barn there, somewhere I used to play as a kid, somewhere I used to take girlfriends to . . . when . . . I was older, you know, teenager . . . I hid my car in there and I . . . went out into the Downs, for . . . I don't know how long . . . I just wandered around . . . I didn't look where I was going, I . . . couldn't think what to do. And I saw it, I saw the solution to all my problems. I saw how to stop hurting the Aged P . . . how to stop hurting Alice . . . how to stop hurting everyone who ever came into contact with me. And I knew what I had to do.

'I went back to the car. There was a hunting knife in the glove compartment, I don't know how long it had been there, left over from some expedition I'd been on. Anyway, I took it. There was a place I knew, used to go blackberrying there as a kid. Knot of trees, surrounded by brambles, nearly impossible to get into. But I did make my way in – that's when I got these.' He rubbed a hand over his thorn-raked face.

'And I knew it was the right place. A body could stay there undiscovered for years, or at least until the next blackberry season. And I knew that was where I would solve my problems.'

There was a silence. Then, with searing self-contempt, he said, 'But when it came to the crunch, I couldn't do it. I put the knife to my throat, I was geared up to do it, but when the moment came, I . . . couldn't do it. I couldn't bring about that simple solution to all the things that are wrong with my life. I was a failure at that, just as I'd always been a failure at everything else.

'So, I threw the knife into the brambles and went back to the car. I drove back here . . . I don't know why . . . maybe to admit to the Aged P how totally I had let him down.'

There was a silence. Then Jude said, 'And presumably, when you came back here, that was the first you knew about Heather's death?'

'Yes. Another disaster, to add to all of the existing disasters.'

Silence again. Then, from Jude, 'I have spoken to Alice, you know.'

'Have you?' He sounded as interested as if she'd mentioned someone he'd never met, in another country.

'She will be so relieved to know that you're all right.'

'All right!' he bellowed suddenly. 'All right? Is this what you call bloody "all right"?'

'Has someone told her?'

'What?'

'That you're still alive?'

'I don't know. The Aged P said she had kept ringing. Maybe he told her.' Again, it was not a matter of consequence to him.

'Roddy . . . Alice did tell me . . . what happened between you at the Craigmullen.'

'Or rather what *didn't* happen between us at the Craigmullen.'

'And I know you blame yourself, but—'

'Of course I bloody blame myself! Who else is there to blame?'

Jude didn't reply at that moment. She knew there was only one answer to his question. Leonard Mallett. But that was a story that would require careful, gradual telling.

'Alice still loves you, and I am sure, with appropriate help, you can get back together and—'

'Get back together to be a laughing stock to the entire bloody world!'

'What do you mean?'

'You wouldn't know, because you've never spent time in an all-male environment like the army. You don't know what men talk about, you don't know the jokes they throw back and forth. Jokes about potency, jokes about being able to keep it up, jokes about wedding night disasters. And they'll find out . . . They certainly will, if Alice is going to go around telling what happened to all and sundry!'

'I am not "all and sundry",' said Jude, uncharacteristically riled. 'Alice told me in confidence, and I can assure you I will never breathe a word about it to another living soul!'

'No?'

'No.' The silence stretched between them. 'Alice does want to see you, you know.'

'Oh, so she's mad too, is she?'

For the first time, Jude thought there might have been a hint of gallows humour in his words. But the idea was abruptly crushed as Roddy roared out, 'Well, I never want to see her again!'

And Jude felt unreasoning fury at the destruction that Leonard Mallett had unleashed.

Twenty-Two

Jude called her friendly cab driver and got him to take her straight to the Shorelands Estate. The Alice who opened the door of Sorrento looked even worse than she had last time they met. Her plump face had hollowed out, there were purple rings beneath her eyes, and her hair had lost touch with a brush for some days. The increased untidiness of the house matched her state.

She drew back listlessly from the doorway to let Jude in.

'I've been to see Roddy.'

'Ah.' The girl didn't seem interested as she drooped her way into the sitting room.

'You did know he'd come back?'

'Yes, his dad called me.' Alice flopped down on to a sofa.

'Well, aren't you pleased?' asked Jude, lowering herself into an armchair.

'Why?'

'He disappeared. Now he's reappeared. Nothing ghastly had happened to him. He's alive. He's safe.'

'Mm.'

'We are talking about your husband, Alice.'

'Oh yes. We're married.' She sounded surprised by the fact. 'We'll have to get that undone, won't we? I wonder if there's an entry in the *Guinness*

Book of Records for the shortest ever marriage. We might be in with a chance for that.'

'Alice,' said Jude with a rare edge of asperity, 'you can't be so negative.'

'Can't I?'

'Look, you've loved Roddy for a long time. And he loves you. All that emotion can't just evaporate in a moment.'

'No?'

'No. All right, at the moment you're both traumatized. Neither of you is in any state to make rational decisions. But that will pass. You'll get better. When you're less stressed, your true feelings will return.'

'"True feelings"? I don't think I've got any true feelings. For the last few months I've been kidding myself that I have, that I was capable of genuine emotion, that I could even be in love. Now I know I was just kidding myself. My true feelings were killed a long time ago. Dad killed them. And he killed my capacity for love.'

'That's not true.'

'How do you know? Oh, of course, you understand human emotions, don't you?' the girl sneered. 'From the lofty heights of your healing?'

'No, that's not how I see it. But from the humble perspective of my healing, I know that people can get better, I know that psychological damage can be undone. I'm not saying it's easy. But it's possible.'

'Huh,' Alice grunted with weary cynicism. 'When Roddy's dad rang, for a moment I might have believed that. I got excited. Roddy was OK.

Maybe we could pick up again, maybe we could sort ourselves out.'

'Yes.'

'But that was before I knew Roddy didn't want to see me again.'

'I'm sure that's not—'

Alice cut through, with a cold hard edge to her voice. 'I asked Mr Skelton if Roddy wanted to see me. He said no. All right, I've done some humiliating things in my time, but I'm not going on bended knee to beg someone to see me, when they've made it perfectly clear they don't want to.'

'Alice, you just need time.'

'Oh yes? I've always been told I need time. Time to train to become a better actress. Time for singing lessons to make me a better singer. But there isn't enough time in the world to prevent me from being what I always have been. A total failure. Someone so broken that I can never be repaired.'

'Just give it a little time, Alice, and—'

'"Time" again! Oh, that's great, coming from you. A healer, and what's the best you can come up with? "Time is a great healer"? Huh.'

'Alice, I'm sure I could persuade Roddy to see you.'

'"Persuade"? That's great. I do have some pride, Jude. I don't want to see my husband simply because someone has *persuaded* him that it's a good idea.'

'That wasn't what I meant.' Jude decided she wasn't getting anywhere on this particular tack. 'Did you get back to Blake Woodruff?'

'What?'

'When I was last here, Blake Woodruff left a message on the machine. I wondered if you'd got back to him.'

'Why should I?'

'Because he knew Heather well. He might know something that would help to reveal why someone would want to kill her.'

'She's dead,' Alice responded with complete indifference. 'Does it really matter who killed her?'

'I would have thought it very definitely did matter.'

'Well, it doesn't matter to me. Not now I know that it wasn't Roddy.'

'How do you know it wasn't Roddy?'

'A couple of the policemen came to see me this morning. To ask more questions.'

'About what?'

'Mostly about Mum's singing lessons with KK Rosser.'

'Oh?' So maybe they were beginning to be suspicions about his alibi. But Jude didn't want to go off in that direction. 'And they told you they didn't think Roddy was involved in the murder?'

'Exactly that. They said they had "eliminated him from their enquiries". And that gave me a lift. I immediately rang Roddy's dad . . . only to get the repeated message that Roddy didn't want to see me.' Tears now flowed unchecked over the girl's smudged mascara.

'And it hasn't occurred to you that Roddy might just be embarrassed at the thought of seeing you . . . given the circumstances under which you last met?'

'No, I'm sure that's not it.' But, even as the words were said, Jude thought she could detect in them a tiny glimmer of hope.

'Alice . . . if you're not going to contact Blake Woodruff, would you mind if I did?'

'I had no arguments with Heather Mallett about anything,' said Bet Harrison. 'When I said I was going to leave the church choir and just concentrate on the Crown & Anchor one, she didn't try to persuade me otherwise, like some of the rest did. She said she thought she might do the same, once the wedding was over. I didn't know her well, but there was certainly no animosity between us. Anyway,' she asked curiously, 'who started you off on this idea, that Heather and I had argued? It sounds to me like it was just someone who wanted to make mischief.'

For the first time, Carole wondered whether this assessment might be right. Elizabeth Browning was such a strange woman, with such a quirky sense of humour, that she might well feel diverting Carole's suspicions towards another choir member was a good joke.

'Go on, who was it?' Bet repeated.

'I'm afraid I can't tell you that. They'd clearly got the wrong end of the stick.'

'I'll say they had.'

They were sitting in Starbucks, the venue where Bet had agreed to meet before her shift there started. Against her better judgement, Carole had been persuaded by the barista to abandon filter coffee and order a black Americano. Against her better judgement, she found she was rather enjoying it.

'I hadn't realized until I moved here,' Bet Harrison observed, 'the level of gossip you get in a place like Fethering. I mean, obviously there was a lot in Evesham, which is where I used to live, but not on this scale. It seems to me that gossip proliferates in inverse proportion to the size of the place where it originated.'

'I think there's a lot of truth in that,' said Carole.

'Whereas there is not a lot of truth in the gossip.'

'Probably not,' she conceded. 'Mind you, a murder on our doorstep is bound to set tongues wagging.'

'So long as they don't wag about the idea that I might have had anything to do with Heather Mallett's death . . .'

'No, obviously not,' said Carole, feeling a little guilty about having followed up on Elizabeth Browning's – probably malicious – hint. But now she'd got Bet Harrison here, she might as well find out what she could from the woman. 'So,' she asked, 'you didn't really know Heather at all, outside the choir context?'

'No. She was perfectly pleasant to me and, when I first moved here, I was glad of any kind of social contact. It's difficult starting from scratch in a new place, which was why I joined the church choir, you know, to meet some people. Then the same with the Crown & Anchor one, which I found worked better for me . . . you know, with my commitments to Rory.'

'Yes. Was he part of the pub choir too?'

'No. I wanted him to join, but his voice has just started breaking and he's very embarrassed about it. I do want him to keep up his singing when his voice has settled down, though. I'm very worried about him not having a social group down here . . . with us having moved so recently. You know we moved after my marriage broke up?'

'Yes, I had heard that.'

'You're divorced too, aren't you, Carole?'

'Yes,' came the reply, in a tone that prohibited further discussion of the subject. Carole moved swiftly on. 'Has Rory always been musical?'

The ploy of getting a mother to talk about the talents of her offspring worked, as it always does. 'Oh yes, from a child,' said Bet. 'He can pick up a tune after one hearing. I think he really could have a future as a professional singer, with the proper training. I asked Jonny Virgo if he would consider giving Rory private lessons, but he said absolutely not. He said he'd taught quite enough singing lessons during his career as a schoolmaster, and he didn't want to do any more of it. He was surprisingly vehement on the subject.

'So, then I asked Heather whether she would recommend KK as a teacher. She said yes, he'd be very good, but the more I saw of him at the Crown & Anchor Choir sessions, the less keen I felt on the idea of Rory spending time with him.'

'Oh?'

'There's something very shifty about KK. I don't trust him. I wouldn't want to spend time alone with him. And I'm sure there was something going on between him and Heather.'

'Hard to know,' suggested Carole, who hadn't seen the pair together as much as Bet had. But the idea of reviving suspicions of KK in the role of murderer was not an unattractive one.

Bet went on, 'Rory's at a very susceptible age. I don't want him to get into bad habits.'

'Are you suggesting that KK might have molested him?'

'Good heavens, no!' Bet almost laughed at the idea, then said, more seriously, 'I just don't want Rory to get into drugs.'

'Brian, it's Jude.'

'Oh, good afternoon,' said the clipped military tones.

'It was good to see you this morning.'

'Likewise.'

'Any change with Roddy?'

'I'm afraid not. I've a horrible feeling he's going to be like this for ever. Like a vegetable – or "traumatized" is probably the word you'd use. He's a real mess. And how he'll manage when I pop my clogs, I daren't begin to imagine. Stuck in some dreadful care home, it doesn't bear thinking of.'

'You mustn't think like that.'

'Damned hard not to, with my son just sitting there like a vegetable.'

'Listen, Brian, I've talked to Alice.'

'Oh, yes?'

'She's in a terrible state too.'

'Well, that doesn't help, does it? Thank God it looks unlikely they'll have children. Any those two produced would be barking, wouldn't they?'

Jude ignored this, and pressed on. 'Alice says that, every time she's rung your house, you've told her Roddy doesn't want to speak to her.'

'Yes.'

'Is that true?'

'Yes, every time she's rung that's what I told her.'

'That wasn't what I meant, Brian. As you know full well. I meant: has he really said that, or have you been trying to protect him?'

There was a silence from the other end of the line. Then he said, 'All right. Roddy hasn't actually said that. I haven't wanted to worry him with Alice's messages. Quite honestly, I think she's the cause of all his troubles. Getting mixed up with a neurotic little madam like that . . . well, if people start having mental problems . . . "he that toucheth pitch shall be defiled." You know what I mean?'

'Yes. I don't agree with you, but I know what you mean. Anyway, what I'm asking is that next time Alice rings, let her speak to Roddy.'

'I can't do that. He's already in a bad enough state. Talking to her might just push him over the edge.'

'It might also help pull him back from the edge. Please,' said Jude. 'Please let him talk to her.'

Twenty-Three

It was the following morning when Jude had a call from Alice Mallett. From the first words, she knew that the girl had been totally transformed.

'I spoke to Roddy,' she said.

'Good. I knew it would help.'

'Oh God, you've no idea just how much it helps! I know there are still huge problems ahead of us, but I think we do have a future.'

'I'm sure you do.'

There was a manic note in the girl's voice as she went on, 'So I've picked myself up and I'm really going to embrace that future. I looked at myself in the mirror after I'd come off the phone from Roddy, and I couldn't believe the state I was in. I've showered and changed and put on some make-up, and I look like a human being again. And the house – I couldn't believe the mess there either. I've cleaned it all over, and opened the windows to let some fresh air in. I'm starting a new life, Jude, as of today. I've even organized a singing lesson for myself, here at the house. He's coming at three this afternoon.'

'Singing lessons? Just like your stepmother.'

'Yes. Just like Mum.'

'That sounds really good,' said Jude, unaware of the renewed suspicion that Bet Harrison had ignited about the activities of KK Rosser.

* * *

'Hello, is that Blake Woodruff?'

'Who is this speaking?'

'My name is Jude. You don't know me, but—'

'If I don't know you, get off the line! I don't know how you got this number, but—'

'I'm a friend of Heather Mallett,' said Jude quickly, before he could slam the phone down. 'And of her stepdaughter Alice.'

'Oh. Oh.' The internationally famous tenor took a moment to adjust his tone from anger to sympathy. 'I was desperately sorry to hear about . . . what happened.'

'Yes. You haven't heard from Alice, have you?' Jude was wondering whether the girl's transformed mood might have encouraged her to catch up on such calls.

'No. No, I left a message at the house. I'd just come back from a tour in Australia.'

'The reason I'm calling you is that Alice is in rather a state.'

'I'm not surprised. I'm still pretty shaken up by the news. And to hear that Heather was murdered . . . Well, you just don't expect that kind of thing to happen to people who, you know, people you've been close to.'

'You met at university, I gather?'

'Right, Manchester. Mutual interest in music brought us together. Sang together in university choirs. We did have a bit of a thing in our last year. I don't know whether it would have gone the distance, but . . . it was very pleasant while it lasted. And then, after we graduated, we went our separate ways. I got increasingly caught up in my career as a professional singer, and Heather

. . . We kept in touch, letters, the occasional phone call, email and Facebook weren't around back then. I'd bring her up to date on my latest disastrous romance, and she . . . well, she always was quite reserved, and she seemed to become more, sort of, turned in on herself. Then, after she got married . . . I wasn't, by the way, invited to the ceremony . . . Anyway, all communication from her ceased. I guess she wanted to make a completely fresh start . . .'

He sounded a bit wistful about the breaking-off of contact. Jude knew it wasn't the moment to say that its cause was probably not Heather's decision, but that of her controlling husband.

'Incidentally . . .' he said, '. . . sorry, what was your name?'

'Jude.'

'Jude, right.' There was a new note of caution in his voice. 'I don't want any of this to get out to the press. They hound me all the bloody time, and if they got hold of the news that I'd once had an affair with a woman who's been murdered . . .'

'I can assure you I have nothing to do with the press. I'm only phoning you on behalf of Alice Mallett. I'm sure she will give you a call herself when she's in a better state.'

'Yes. Yes, fine. Sorry to have sounded so suspicious, but someone in my position has to be bloody careful.'

'I'm sure you do. I fully understand.'

'Good. Yes. You haven't heard about the funeral details yet, have you? If the press can be kept at bay, I'd like to put in an appearance then.'

'There's no news about that yet. I think in the case of a murder, it takes a while for the police to release the body.' Jude didn't know that for sure, but she thought she was probably right.

'Yes, of course. Well, when you do hear something . . .'

'Either Alice or I will let you know.'

'Thank you.'

'Incidentally, Blake, did you hear that Heather's husband had died?'

'I heard that, yes. From Heather. She got back in touch with me. She didn't talk much about it, but I got the impression that it may not have been a marriage made in heaven.' Something of an understatement, thought Jude. 'But she suggested meeting up, for old times' sake. Which I would have been happy to do, but my bloody schedule, what with concerts here, and the occasional opera and foreign tours . . . I get booked more than a year ahead, would you believe, so making social arrangements can be a nightmare.' He didn't speak in a boastful way, he was just describing one of the hazards of his profession.

'And now,' he concluded sadly, 'that "old times' sake" meeting with Heather will never happen.'

'No.' There was a moment of reflective silence, before Jude asked, 'Was there anything else Heather talked to you about, you know, in the past few months, after her husband's death . . .?'

Carole had by now got the bit between her teeth and was determined to increase her contribution to the investigation – or, ideally, to solve the murder on her own. Her direct approach to

Elizabeth Browning had not been an unqualified success, but the direct approach to Bet Harrison had proved more fruitful. At least it showed her the direction in which her next enquiries should go.

She had a copy of that week's *Fethering Observer*, with a photograph of Heather Mallett on the front, and among the small ads, the regular entry was still there. She rang the mobile number that was printed in the box.

Her call was greeted by a laid-back 'Hi.'

'Am I talking to KK Rosser?'

'You are. Guitarist *extraordinaire*. Leader of Rubber Truncheon, the best undiscovered and unsigned band this side of Memphis. Available for any kind of gig – weddings, birthdays, bar mitzvahs, hen parties, divorce parties – you name it, we'll provide the best evening of music you've heard since Woodstock. So, what is the occasion for which you require our services?'

'Actually, I saw your advertisement in the *Fethering Observer* for singing lessons.' Carole planned to start with a conventional enquiry before moving on to the meat of her investigation.

'Oh, right. Well, that's a turn-up.'

'Why?'

'Well, because I get so few enquiries about the singing lessons. Lots for Rubber Truncheon, of course.' He was probably lying. 'But very few for the old singing lessons. Haven't had an enquiry about that for . . . ooh, six months at least.'

'Well, actually, that wasn't what I really wanted to ask you about.'

'Oh?'

Carole now decided that she should use a little subterfuge by pretending that she wasn't totally retired from the Home Office. 'The fact is, I'm making enquiries into the death of Heather Mallett.'

The line went dead.

'Oh, general chat, you know,' Blake Woodruff replied. 'Heather told me what Alice was up to, all about the forthcoming wedding, that kind of stuff.'

'Did she say anything about her late husband?'

'His name wasn't mentioned. Which, when I think about it, was perhaps rather odd. But I didn't think that at the time. We only had a few telephone conversations, didn't talk that much.'

'And did Heather seem to have changed from when you'd last been in touch?'

'She did a bit, yes.'

'In what way?'

'Well, as I say, she always had a reclusive tendency, and that seemed to be more pronounced in our recent conversations. There was a kind of hesitancy about her, as if she was afraid something she said might upset me.'

The product of years spent with the permanently critical Leonard, thought Jude. 'Nothing else, nothing odd?'

'No, I don't think so . . . Oh, there was one thing . . .'

'What?'

'Nothing odd, really. Just a coincidence.'

'Oh?'

'She'd met someone in Fethering who I'd known years ago.'

'Who was that?'

'I don't know if you know, but I started out life . . . well, no, I'd done a little bit of living before that . . . but, at a very young age, I became a choral scholar at a cathedral school. Yes, I'm afraid the music bug has been with me for a long, long time. And it turns out that the master in charge of the choir back then . . . was choir-master for the church choir in Fethering, who Heather sang with.'

'Jonny Virgo?'

'Yes, "Mr Virgo" to us back then. Mind you, that didn't stop a lot of smutty-minded little boys making jokes about his surname. Anyway, I told Heather I remembered him, and I asked if he remembered me, you know, if he'd mentioned my name. And she said no. Which I thought slightly odd, because when someone has the good fortune to become famous, as I have had, then all sorts of people come out of the woodwork, claiming that they gave him his first job, they recognized his exceptional potential at a very early age, that they taught him everything he knew. But old Mr Virgo apparently didn't do that. He didn't claim to have taught me everything I knew.'

'More than that,' said Jude, remembering a rehearsal in All Saints. 'He positively denied that he knew you and moved the conversation on very quickly when your name came up.'

'Yes, Heather told me that. And at first, I couldn't think of any reason for it. And then a memory came back to me.'

'A memory of what?'

'A memory of Mr Virgo telling me he loved me.'

'What?'

'It was the end of a choir rehearsal. The other choristers had gone from the chapel, off to supper, I think. It was just Mr Virgo and me, collecting up the hymn books. And he suddenly looked at me, and he said, "I love you, Woodruff." Just that.'

'Did he touch you?'

'No. And it was never mentioned again. And I forgot about it.'

'You didn't tell anyone? Your headmaster or . . .?'

'Oh, for God's sake, no! You didn't in those days. I was . . . what . . . nine? I didn't know what love meant. I knew I loved the family cat – that was about the extent of it. And it didn't damage me in later life. I may have had a few romantic disasters on the way, partly to do with the amount I have to travel, but all of my disasters have been firmly heterosexual. So, Mr Virgo telling me he loved me had absolutely no effect at all on my life.'

'It might have had a bigger effect on his life.'

'Yes, OK, probably did. Maybe that was the first time he had faced the fact that he was gay, the first time he recognized that he could feel love for a small boy. I don't know.'

'But did Heather know about your encounter in the chapel?'

'Yes. I told her while we were at university. You know, when you first have sex with someone, you tell each other about any previous sexual encounters . . . well, to be accurate, you give the other person an edited version of your previous sexual encounters, and I did tell Heather about Mr Virgo being in love with me, told her about it as a joke, really.'

'Did she mention it in one of your more recent conversations?'

'Oh yes.'

'Did she say if she told anyone else about it?'

'She said she'd told Alice.'

'Had she?'

Jude went straight round to High Tor. It took a while before she could tell her story, because Carole was so keen to bring her up to date with the progress of her own investigations. But eventually Jude was able to report the conversation she had just had with Blake Woodruff.

'What do you think that means?' asked Carole.

'I think it means that Alice may potentially be in as much danger as her stepmother was. We must see she's looked after.'

'And we must tell the police to have a word with Jonny Virgo,' said Carole, in her best Home Office voice.

'Yes.' Jude glanced at her watch. 'At least we know Alice is all right at the moment.'

'Oh?'

'She told me she'd booked a three o'clock singing lesson with KK Rosser.'

'But,' said Carole slowly, 'I spoke to KK Rosser this morning. He hasn't had any enquiries about singing lessons for more than six months.' Jude looked at her, aghast. 'Which must mean that Alice is having her singing lesson with someone else.'

Twenty-Four

Carole had never before broken the speed limit on Fethering seafront, but all caution was abandoned in the Renault's dash to the Shorelands Estate. And, once inside the enclave, she certainly must have broken many of the local regulations as she screeched to a halt outside Sorrento.

The front door was locked.

'Shall I ring the bell?' asked Carole.

'No, round the back!' Jude led the way, at a speed surprising for a woman of her bulk.

It was as she had hoped. In her bid to let fresh air into the house, Alice had opened the sitting room's French windows.

They heard the singing first. 'Nymphs and Shepherds', in Alice's pure soprano.

Then they saw her through the windows, sitting at her stepmother's baby grand, accompanying herself from memory. She seemed unaware of the man behind her, carefully loosening the cravat around his neck, preparatory to tightening it around hers.

'Stop it!' Carole bellowed.

He looked up mildly at the two approaching woman. 'Ah,' said Jonny Virgo. 'Rather too much to hope that I would get away with it twice.'

Shortly afterwards they were seated on the chintzy three-piece suite. Alice had made tea and served it in her stepmother's best bone china. What a very genteel, Fethering way to hold a conversation with a murderer.

'I knew I had to,' said Jonny, his cravat once again neatly around his neck. 'I became obsessed by it. Heather knew, and I felt certain that it was only a matter of time before she would tell someone. I had to stop her.'

'So, what did you do?' asked Carole.

'I gave Mother a sleeping pill. She doesn't always sleep well, wakes up not knowing what time of day or night it is, but the sleeping pills do work. So, I knew she'd be dead to the world for a while. And what I was going to do wouldn't take long. Then, knowing that the music for the dancing in the church hall would have to stop at ten thirty, I went down there and waited until Heather came out. I had to wait quite a while.' He sounded aggrieved at the delay. 'People are very long-winded about saying their goodbyes, particularly after a few drinks.

'But finally, Heather came out on her own. I knew she was the last one, because she locked up the hall. Presumably, she would return the key the next day.' A troublesome thought struck him. 'Oh dear. I wonder what happened to the key. It'll be very inconvenient if they can't find it, you know, next time the place is booked.'

'I'm sure they've got a spare,' said Jude.

'Yes, I hope so.' He sounded more worried about the missing key than the crime he'd committed.

'Then what happened?' asked Carole, quite sharply.

'Well, I said "Good evening" to Heather, and

said I was just taking a late-night stroll, and I'd see her a bit of the way home. She was in a very happy state, very pleased with the way the day had gone, extravagantly flattering to me about the music.' A strange little smile hovered on his lips. 'I was glad that her last thoughts were happy ones.'

He saw that no one else was smiling and went on hastily. 'As you know, if you were going from All Saints to the Shorelands Estate, you'd follow the river down to the Fethering Yacht Club. And that's the way we went. Down there, as you also know, there's the sea wall at the mouth of the Fether.'

I was right about the Scene of the Crime, Carole told herself. But the thought didn't bring her much satisfaction.

'I knew that's where I had to do it. I'd slipped off my cravat in readiness. I think she was too surprised to resist when I put it round her neck. She died very quickly. It wasn't easy lifting her body over the sea wall, but I managed it,' he concluded with an air of satisfaction.

There was a silence.

'It was what Heather said after the wedding ceremony, wasn't it?' asked Jude. 'The reason you killed her. When she was talking about Alice knowing Blake Woodruff's secrets, knowing about "everyone who's ever been in love with him" . . .?'

'Yes,' Jonny admitted. 'I knew she wasn't really talking about Alice. I'd followed Blake's career all the way from when he was a chorister. I knew that he and Heather had had a . . . thing while they were at university. And, from when I first met her, I was worried she might mention something about Blake. What she said in the church hall made me certain that she knew what I'd . . . what I'd said to him. I thought she was challenging me with the information. I thought she was threatening to tell everyone about it.'

Jude sighed. To think that such a trivial misunderstanding could have led to a woman's death.

Other details fell into place, though. Carole remembered Bet Harrison saying how vehemently Jonny had been against the idea of giving singing lessons to Rory Harrison. Throughout his career, he must have avoided any situation that might leave him alone with a young boy.

'I couldn't let Mother find out,' Jonny went on. 'She'd always had this image of me as . . . It would have killed her.'

'But why,' asked Carole, 'once you'd silenced Heather, did you feel the need to silence Alice too?'

'It just got to me,' Jonny replied. 'Once Heather had died, I felt a kind of peace. I thought the danger had gone. But then, as the days went by, I felt less and less secure. I knew Heather and Alice were close. Increasingly, I started to think that Heather must have confided in her, passed on what Blake had told her. I couldn't relax, I didn't know what to do . . . and then I had the call from Alice, asking me to come here to give her a singing lesson, and it was like a sign to me.' He spoke as if his actions had been dictated by an ineluctable logic.

There were a lot of things that Jude wanted to say. That, in this day and age, nobody cared about anyone else's sexuality. That what he'd said to the young Blake Woodruff did not constitute an offence.

But she was dealing with someone from a different generation, someone who'd grown up at the time when homosexual acts were still criminal. Jonny Virgo's overriding sense of guilt had prevented him, right through his life, from any kind of sexual expression.

And, most ironic of all, he was someone whose mother was way beyond understanding any charge levelled against him. He was trying to protect her from information she no longer had any means of processing. Jonny Virgo's murder of Heather Mallett – and his attempted murder of Alice Mallett – had been completely unnecessary acts. But he would never understand that.

Carole looked at her watch. 'The police said they'd be here within the half-hour.'

'Yes.' Jonny Virgo nodded, with something approaching satisfaction. 'At least I've finished my recordings,' he said.

'Recordings?' echoed Jude.

'I've been recording all the Beethoven piano sonatas . . . for Mother to listen to . . . if I have to go somewhere else.'

Jude realized that he was quite as out of touch with the real world as Mrs Virgo was. They had lived all their lives, just the two of them, in a capsule of togetherness.

She looked across at Alice Mallett, transfixed by the man who had killed her much-adored stepmother. On the girl's face there was no anger, only pity.

Twenty-Five

'Roddy. Someone to see you.'

Jude spoke from the doorway to the sitting room. Brian Skelton had 'thought it might be a good idea' if he went and did some shopping. So, Jude was the only witness to Roddy and Alice's reunion.

The bride brought up a chair to sit beside her groom. He touched her hand briefly, and she didn't recoil. But both knew they had a long journey to travel.

'I know people who can help you,' said Jude. 'I really do.'

It was surprising how quickly Fethering gossip accommodated the arrest of Jonny Virgo. A lot of people, it turned out, had deduced some time before that he was the murderer. Barney Poulton, in his favourite role as a buttonholing Ancient Mariner, assured an increasingly glassy-eyed Ted Crisp – and indeed anyone else at the bar of the Crown & Anchor – that he had 'known all along.'

At his trial, Jonny Virgo admitted killing Heather Mallett. He was sentenced to life and, once inside, made himself popular by playing piano for all of the prison entertainments. He also formed a reciprocated attachment for a fellow prisoner. Though there was no physical contact, he had finally found a way of expressing his true emotions. They remained a very devoted couple to the end of their incarcerated lives. Their only worry, that one would inevitably be released before the other, was not realized because they both died, within days of each other, before the end of their sentences.

Jonny's mother made little demur when she was moved to a care home which had a view of the sea on the front at Fethering. So long as she had her CD player, on which to listen to her beloved son playing the Beethoven piano concertos, she asked no more of life.

The Rev. Bob Hinkley's efforts at controlling events in his parish led him to a nervous breakdown. When he recovered, he left the church and went back into industry. And nobody in Fethering ever knew what that 'industry' was. His replacement as vicar decided that, given All Saints' dwindling congregation, it could no longer support a church choir. Recorded music was introduced to services.

Ruskin Dewitt continued to be the life and soul of parties that nobody really wanted him to attend. And he sang, as flatly as ever, in the choir of All Souls Fedborough.

Bet Harrison found a new man, and her son Rory discovered girls.

Elizabeth Browning continued to go on about Glyndebourne and her nodules, and to maintain her lonely seaside vigils, which still proved a very good way of picking up men.

KK Rosser got fewer and fewer gigs for Rubber Truncheon. And no one asked him to give them singing lessons. Nor did he or anyone else revive the Crown & Anchor Choir.

Roddy and Alice Skelton did consult the therapist whom Jude had recommended and worked very hard with him to come to terms with their different problems. The success of the treatment could be measured by the fact that they became the parents of three healthy children. Brian Skelton lived long enough to meet the first of these, but then, with characteristic stoicism – and 'no fuss' – succumbed to bowel cancer.

His son, daughter-in-law and grandchildren lived in Sorrento on the Shorelands Estate and, when they were in their teens, the youngsters joined the Fethering Yacht Club.

That did not mean, however, that Roddy and Alice's lives were all plain sailing. Though things got better, both remained damaged, one by the war in Afghanistan, the other by the attentions of Leonard Mallett. They still had setbacks and advances. Such people's stories may get better, but they do not have fairy-tale endings.

And, true to her word, Jude never told anyone – least of all Carole – the true circumstances of Leonard Mallett's death. To her mind, and according to her scale of values, justice had been done.

One weekend that autumn, Carole had her granddaughters, Lily and Chloe, to stay. Among the excitements lined up for them was Sunday lunch with Granny's next-door neighbour Jude. After the little girls had stuffed themselves with sausages, baked beans and oven chips, and the adults enjoyed local Sole Mornay (with lavish amounts of New Zealand Sauvignon Blanc), Jude said she'd tidy the kitchen while Carole read a story to her charges.

The book chosen was *The Wheels on the Bus*. Lily knew she was really too grown-up for it, but she did love hearing her baby sister trying to join in with the words. It made her feel very proud of her superior language skills.

Carole was so involved that, unwittingly, she found herself leading the singing.

The wheels on the bus go round and round,
Round and round, round and round.
The wheels on the bus go round and round,
All day long.

When she and the girls came to a more-or-less unison close, Carole looked up to see her neighbour in the kitchen doorway, with an amused smile on her face.

'What's the matter?' she asked.

'You know, Carole,' said Jude, 'that was in tune.'